The Vatican is a real place and is described as best as possible but used fictitiously in this novel. The same is true of eating places, airports and other places frequented by characters in this novel.

In all other respects, however, this novel is a work of fiction. Names, characters, places and incidents are either the product of the author's imagination or are used fictitiously. Any resemblance to actual persons, living or dead, or to actual events or locales is unintentional and coincidental.

The Pope from Peoria

A fiction of a Pope's desire to break the stained glass ceiling for women in the Church

First Edition Design Publishing
Sarasota, Florida USA

The Pope from Peoria

ISBN 978-1506-903-06-4 PRINT
ISBN 978-1506-903-07-1 EBOOK

LCCN 2016953968

September 2016

Published and Distributed by
First Edition Design Publishing, Inc.
P.O. Box 20217, Sarasota, FL 34276-3217
www.firsteditiondesignpublishing.com

Acknowledgements

I have to acknowledge my good friends who spent their time and expertise reading and editing this story.

A good friend Joyce that took time from her work – and golf – to read this fiction. She even had a name suggestion for one of the characters.

Members of our Church choir, Joanne, Cecilia and Karen giving me many corrections and suggestions.

Jack, another friend and member of our Church Social Justice committee, who constantly kept prodding me to keep going.

My brother Ed, a very pragmatic individual, who not only found typos but asked the good questions like, "Who is speaking now?" and "What are you talking about in this sentence?"

And finally my wife Clara, who patiently read and re-read many phrases and sentences without getting perturbed with her bothersome husband.

PROLOGUE

It was a hot July afternoon in Italy. A doctor had been called to pronounce the death of the Pope. The death occurred quite suddenly while the Pope was at the summer residence of Castal Gandolfo about twenty miles from Rome. Due to the nature of the Pope's heart conditions, a sudden death had been predicted and he had no chance to make any of his wishes known except to be buried in the earth as some of his predecessors had been buried. He did not want to be buried in a sarcophagus (stone coffin). There was some confusion, but his death was expected to occur quite quickly. Two of his siblings and some resident Cardinals stood around at his bedside. They stepped back as Cardinal Josip Perez, the current Cardinal-Camerlengo, and the most senior Cardinal, proceeded to unofficially pronounce death.In early days a mirror was placed near the dying Pope's mouth or nose to ascertain death. Even though now in modern times a doctor officially pronounces death, the Cardinal-Camerlengo removed a small silver mallet from a red, leather pouch and tapped the Pope gently three times on the forehead and called his birth name. The Cardinal announced, "The Pope is dead."

At this point a great amount of activity had begun. The Prefect of the Papal Household now had many necessary preparations to make. St. Martha's House with its 130 rooms will house the Cardinals. This is an apartment complex for the Cardinals. Transportation must be arranged from here to the Sistine Chapel. Once the Conclave is secured no one is allowed to approach the Cardinals as they travel between the two buildings. Even if they pass some of the groundkeepers, they are forbidden to speak to them. In 1996, Pope John Paul in an Apostolic Constitution called Universi Dominici Gregis (UDG), published norms to regulate the election of successors. Popes often make small adjustment to the burial procedures responding to their desires.

The Vatican Press and thirty or more other news agencies throughout the world will cover the procedure. There will be many predictions as to who will be the next Pope. The mournful tears of the thousands of faithful in Rome will turn to tears of joy when the new Pope is elected. The bell of Arco Campani rang the Pope's death knell. All bells of the city rang as well.

The body of the Pope will continue to lie in state in the Hall of the Swiss Guard at Castal Gandolfo. The body will be guarded day and night by the Swiss Guard and members of the Papal Household. Several Franciscans are arriving to chant the Office of the Dead before the body is transferred to Rome. A motorcycle police escort will lead the funeral procession through the villa's Gate of the Moor. Twenty-five autos transporting relatives and close friends will follow along the Via Appia Nuova to St. John Lateran, the basilica of the Bishop of Rome. Once here the body of the Pope will remain in the hearse while the Franciscans pray the Office of the Dead. After a final blessing the procession will continue to St. Peter's Basilica to be viewed by thousands of mourners.

As the hearse enters the square, the Italian Honor Guard and Swiss Guard will snap into a salute. Forty-two Cardinals dressed in bright red and carrying lighted candles, will assist in placing the coffin at the steps of the world's largest church. Accompanying the body will be black-robed Third Order Franciscan confessors, white surpliced priests and family. The body will then be carried into St. Peter's Basilica. According to previous press reports, the death of a pope usually brings approximately three million mourners in ten days to pass the bier.

The Cardinal-Secretary of State and other senior officials will have much to do. Thousands of the faithful, and the curious, will gather in St. Peter's Square. There will be many colorful banners and flags scattered throughout the multitudes. There will even be some betting on who will be the next Pope. Odds favor the senior Cardinal, Josip Perez.

The pope had no opportunity to either give a final assessment of the needs of the Church or give any recommendation of who should replace him. This advice was seldom heeded even though his counsel was sought as a courtesy. Pope John Paul VI wrote the latest rules for the election of a successor to a Pope. He said 120 to be the maximum number of Cardinals. To discuss the needs of the Church a General Congregation will be held to discuss those needs. Some of the items discussed will be the handling of funeral expenses and the destruction of the deceased Pope's fisherman's ring. Even the die used to make lead seals for apostolic letters is destroyed.

The Cardinals throughout the world were very aware that the Pope's death would happen suddenly. Some were already in Rome and many others had contingent plans arranged for a quick flight to the Vatican. The remaining few others are feverishly making plans to fly to Rome. None of the Cardinals want to be left out of the upcoming Conclave. A few of the Cardinals were already planning how to jockey into a position to be elected the next Pope. Even these holy men of the Church found it hard sometimes to be humble. They may not be able to influence the Holy Spirit but they surely could sway some of the voting Cardinals. Before the Conclave, the Cardinals will meet in the Pauline Chapel of the Apostolic Palace to pray for enlightenment from the Holy Spirit. From there they will proceed to the Sistine Chapel.

All officials of the Holy See lose their power and position until the new Pope reinstates them or nominates new ones. Cardinal-Camerlengo Perez will temporally serve the Church as administrator during the Sede Vacante. The Pope, as did the previous Pope, requested a simple burial in the Earth. The Camerlengo will accommodate his wishes. The body of the Pope will be vested in the white simar of the pope, a white alb, cincture and amice. The pallium, symbolizing his universal authority will be placed around his neck. Again, symbolizing the privilege of Popes, the golden mitre will be placed on his head. As is the custom, three coffins will be used, one inside the other. One will be of cypress, signifying the Pope is a simple man, the second is of lead, engraved with the name of the Pontiff, and placed inside are copies of important issues, and the third coffin is of elm, the most precious wood available in Rome.

At this time, accommodations are being arranged in the close-quartered Sistine Chapel for the Conclave to meet and elect a new

Pope. The Conclave must begin no earlier than fifteen days and no later than twenty days after the death of the Pope. The Pope is the leader of over one billion Catholics throughout the world, of which one million are in Rome to await the announcement of the new Pope.

CHAPTER ONE

Monday morning, nineteen days after the death of the Pope, Cardinal Perez, the Cardinal-Camerlengo,called all Cardinals presently in Rome to a meeting. The Cardinal was a short, five feet, six inches tall and almost completely bald. His bushy eye brows made up for his baldness. His rotund shape was similar to a bowling pin. He was known to have a quick temper. The Cardinal was born in Spain which accounted for his Italian conversation having a Spanish accent. At age 59, he was one of the youngest Cardinal-Camerlengo in Vatican history. It was a mystery how he maneuvered himself up through the ranks to his current position so quickly. Speculation was he used various devious means to achieve that goal. He is also currently the Secretary of State of the Vatican.

The Pope's sudden death caused some confusion and delay in organizing the Conclave. Except for the Cardinals living at the Vatican, the other Cardinals seldom got together except for Conclaves. Since several were new Cardinals, some were not acquainted with each other. The Church had been without a leader for eighteen days. They used this time to discuss their choices for a leader and what problems needed to be addressed. Being human, some of the dialogue became heated. Disagreements ranged from the deceased Pope's appointments of new Cardinals to assignments to even new Church rules.

Talking to the assembled Cardinals, Cardinal Perez said, "Without further delay, we must make arrangements for the Conclave." Although he tried to conceal his desire to be Pope someday, most Cardinals were keenly aware of it. Displaying some impatience in his voice, he said, "I have directed that the Sistine Chapel be made ready with chairs and tables. The Swiss

Guard is currently barring the entrance to the courtyard. I have also directed that the quarters of Domus Sanctae Marthae (St. Martha's House) be prepared for the other Cardinals arriving in Rome for the Conclave." All Cardinals had not yet arrived in Rome after the Pontiff's death.

Since it was now the morning of the nineteenth day since the death of the Pontiff, the Conclave had an urgent responsibility to fulfill. Under Michelangelo's beautiful hand-painted frescoes in the Sistine Chapel, 116 Cardinals crowd in to elect a new Pope. In addition to Michelangelo's paintings many other frescoes surrounded the room looking down on the Cardinals. Two ballots would be taken to the sickly Cardinals remaining in their rooms. They each sat at their cramped little chairs placed around twelve long tables arranged along the walls. Name tags were placed for each Cardinal. In previous Conclaves canopies were placed over each cardinal. The prior Pope discontinued the practice. The tables were covered with beige and maroon felt. Elbow to elbow, they could easily see what the other Cardinal was writing if so desired. Like school children they hid their writing from their neighbor. Although all the Cardinals knew the procedure, Cardinal Perez announced "There will be two votes this morning and two this afternoon until a Pope is selected." The prior Pope can alter this voting process as he wishes.

Amber light seemed to radiate in all directions in the Chapel as did the stifling heat. As more of a formality, the doors were sealed with ribbon and wax. It was not hermetically sealed as assumed. Still in mourning the Cardinals entered the Conclave to choose a Pope. Taking an oath of absolute secrecy, the Cardinals took their small seats around the Chapel. The secrecy oath is almost a foolhardy effort since, even though all doors are locked, the Cardinals voices can be heard by anyone standing near the doors and cracks of the old edifice. These cracks in the building expand and contract greatly with temperature. The Swiss Guards are the only ones allowed at the doors and most often they can hear the voices of the Cardinals. All voting Cardinals must be under the age of eighty. Older Cardinals may not remain in the chapel. Since it is almost twenty days since the death of the Pope, there is some sense of urgency. During these days of General Congregations, sermons are given at titular Churches regarding what kind of Pope is needed. Many of the Cardinals began conversing with each other, giving their choice for the Pope and why they think he would be a good candidate.

The Cardinal Camerlengo has asked if there are any questions about procedures or if there are any needs or medical necessities.

"We will choose nine Cardinals at random, "said Cardinal Perez. Though all Cardinals know the procedure, Cardinal Perez announced the rules as if the Cardinals didn't know. He thoroughly enjoyed his position of authority. "Three of the nine will be 'scrutineers' (voting judges), three will collect votes from our ill Cardinals unable to be present in the Chapel, and three will be revisers to check the work of the scrutineers. And, as is the custom, try to disguise your handwriting."

Two non-Cardinals are designated as Masters of Ceremonies. They must leave at the start of the session. They too must take a solemn oath of secrecy just as the Cardinals. The Conclave can then begin its work.

With a few whispers being heard, the ballots were handed out. The paper ballot is rectangular and on the top half is printed "Eligo in Summum Pontificem" (I elect as the most high pontiff). On the lower half of the ballot the Cardinals began writing the name of the person they chose once the non-Cardinals leave the chapel. The Cardinals, secretly but legibly, wrote their choice as pope and folded the ballot. At this time, ballots from Cardinals too ill to attend were collected and brought into the room. Now each Cardinal proceeded to the altar holding up their folded ballot so all can see. Each one said, "I call as my witness Christ the Lord who will be my judge that my vote is given to the one who before God I think should be elected." They placed the ballots on a paten, pierced with a threaded needle and deposited them into the large chalice or urn. The ballots from the ill Cardinals were also added to the urn.

"Begin the procedure," said Cardinal Perez, impatience showing in his voice.

The first scrutineer took the chalice and shook the contents. He solemnly deposited them into the large urn. Then he counted them as he did so to assure the number of ballots corresponded to the number of Cardinals present. If the numbers do not agree, they are all burned and another vote is taken. Each scrutineer examined the folded ballots with the last scrutineer calling out the name on the ballot.

The first scrutineer, Cardinal Francis Madelo, removed a ballot. Opening it, he read it. Looking somewhat perplexed, he handed it to the second scrutineer. Cardinal Ivan Flanis read it and looked around. He handed it to Cardinal Carlo Casterz, who too seemed in a quandary.

Growing more impatient, Cardinal Perez said, "What's the matter? Read the name."

Cardinal Casterz looked up. "There seems to be a problem."

"How can there be a problem? Just read the name."

Cardinal Casterz handed the ballot back to the second scrutineer, Cardinal Flanis. "You read it."

"There's no reason to stall!" said Cardinal Perez. "Just read the name!"

Cardinal Flanis read the name. "William Joseph von Meier III."

Cardinal Perez jumped up and grabbed the ballot. Looking at the ballot he said, "This is an atrocity! Who did this?"

The Cardinals looked around, squirming in their seats.

"I ask in the Name of our Lord, who submitted this name?" again asked Cardinal Perez.

No one raised their hand.

"The man who wrote this is standing on the verge of excommunication. You are making a farce of the Holy Spirit. Who submitted this name?"

Again no one came forward.

Almost yelling, Cardinal Perez said, "Put it aside! Cardinal Madelo. Read the next ballot, please. I will find out who did this."

"Should I pierce it with the needle?" said the scrutineer.

"NO!" said Cardinal Perez.

Cautiously, Cardinal Madelo reached into the urn and brought out another ballot. Reading it, he quickly threw it back into the urn. He brought out a third ballot, read it and put it back into the urn.

"Is something wrong, Cardinal Madelo?" said Cardinal Perez. The Cardinal took out a fourth, then a handful. "They are all the same, your Eminence. All say William Joseph von Meier III."

"What do you mean? That can't be!"

All the Cardinals again shifted nervously in their seats, the heat of the room even more stifling.

Almost yelling, Cardinal Perez said, "Is this a conspiracy? What's going on? Don't you gentlemen realize the seriousness of our task? God, the Holy Spirit, has entrusted us in the sacred task. Why are you doing this?"

Cardinal Johnson stood up and took out several of the ballots. "They all have a William Joseph von Meier III on them," he said.

The Cardinals began to murmur. Someone yelled out, "God is speaking to us!"

Another said, "God doesn't speak this way to us."

"It's the work of the devil," another Cardinal said.

Trying to regain order Cardinal Perez said, "Someone is playing a cruel trick on us. I will immediately have our electronic experts examine this Chapel. We will dispense with today's voting. The paper of the ballots will be checked as will be the ink. We will then burn the ballots and I want you to return to your rooms and say nothing to anyone. Call the Swiss Guards in here. I want to find out if any unauthorized persons have been in the Chapel this morning."

"What chemicals should I color the smoke?" asked Cardinal Rezinsky. There were two stoves, one the electric auxiliary stove with a red start button. It was used to get the other stove started. As a result of the two flues connected in a wye, smoke often backed up into the room. Also the color of smoke was usually hard to distinguish. Even with the proper chemical canisters it was not easy to get the correct color of smoke. Also if the flue was not up to the proper temperature, smoke would sometimes back up into the chapel. Even opening the stove door to add more ballots caused smoke to belch into the room. Electing a pope happened so seldom, no one ever practiced using the stove.

"What do you think? Black, and don't let the smoke back up in the Chapel," yelled Cardinal Perez.

"It's windy today, Josip."

"Shut up!"

With that, the Cardinals silently and solemnly filed out of the Sistine Chapel. Those observing, standing outside the Chapel, knew something was wrong. The smoke seemed to be dark gray. Down through the centuries the Cardinals knew the Faithful had a limited amount of patience waiting for the announcement of a new Pope. The Press, the Clergy, the crowd of visitors knew the new Pope would have many dilemmas and crises to quell so they were eager to have a new Pope elected.

The Church was losing members at an alarming rate and others were falling away or not practicing their faith. There was the problem of millions Catholics that just did not take an active part in services. They readily called themselves Catholics but hardly ever attended Mass other than Christmas or Easter. A study by the University of Turin found 80% of Romans say they are Catholics but 70% approve birth control, divorce, cohabitation and pre-marital sex. Less than half believe in an afterlife.

And the Church just does not excite the youth to be active members. Evangelistic denominations were growing at a disquieting proportion. Many of these services gave the appearance of a rock concert and the young people seemed to be drawn to them. Just as youngsters did in kindergarten, the twenty to thirty year old members were drawn to the bright, colorful music, videos and sparkling and witty homilies by energetic ministers. The new Pope would have a hefty job ahead of him.

If you enjoyed the story, tell your friends on face book or where ever. It's available in book form and e book on Amazon.com. If you were too shocked, tell them anyway.

CHAPTER TWO

For the rest of the morning Cardinal Perez with several of the resident electricians, electronic and computer staff began examining the Chapel. As they had done days earlier in normal preparation, they looked for hidden cameras, microphones and any other type of electronic jamming devices. So many wires and cables crisscrossed the room; the floor had to be raised one meter to accommodate the wiring and the jamming devices. Sadly, a carpeted false floor covered the beautiful marble pavement.

Giovanni Menzotti, the chief electrician said, "Why are we looking for a camera? The trick was done in or under the urn. The ballots were probably doctored."

"I'm sure whoever did this wanted to see our faces," said Cardinal Perez. "They wanted to see our expressions. I've called the Vatican Police."

"Cardinal Perez, there is no hole in the urn," said another staff member. "And there is no hole in the chalice or even the table."

Angrily Cardinal Perez said, "Look under the table for a false bottom!"

A husky and bearded electrician Anthony Medina crawled under the table. He whispered to another worker, "I bet it's a mutiny," he grunted as he lifted his large body back up. "There's no hole, your Eminence," he said to the Cardinal. Anthony whispered to another worker, "Our Church is in such disarray."

"Don't you dare let the Cardinal hear you say that," said a balding Vito Desgatino.

Cardinal Madelo walked into the Chapel and watched the flurry of activity. "Josip, you do realize this is the twentieth day since our beloved Pope died?" he said as he seated himself in a chair. He was sweating profusely in the heat of an Italian summer.

Sweat was seeping through his garments. "I wish our beloved Pope had died in the winter."

"You will address me as 'your Eminence'," said Cardinal Perez.

"Sure I will, Josip," said Cardinal Madelo, with an emphasis on 'Josip'. The Cardinals do not normally address each other as "Your Eminence".

Ignoring the remark, Cardinal Perez said, "We'll have another vote this afternoon."

"I have a feeling you and your crew won't find anything," said Cardinal Madelo.

"And why not?" said Cardinal Perez.

Cardinal Madelo remained silent.

By noon, Stefan, the assistant chief staff electrician said, "Your Eminence, we haven't found anything unusual about the Chapel. We have checked for any radio frequency signals or digital pulses. The Chapel is clean."

Cardinal Perez stood at the altar with his hands on his hips. "I have to say prayers. Have everyone here in the Chapel by two. This time we'll do a proper vote. Ask if anyone has seen any of those flying things hovering near the Chapel. You know, with cameras on them? "

"You mean drones?"

"Whatever they are called."

"No, your Eminence. We haven't seen any such thing."

With that the Cardinal stormed out of the room.

Once again the Cardinals seated themselves around the Sistine Chapel. Two different non-Cardinals prepared to hand out the ballots. Cardinal Perez assigned three different scrutineers also.

"Brethren in Christ, I cannot explain what happened today. I don't want to think all of you would...let's say mutiny. I hope all have prayed fervently to the Holy Spirit. All of the Faithful are waiting for our vote for our new Holy Father. Let's not disappoint them. Let us say an *Our Father*, a *Hail Mary* and a *Glory Be* and begin our vote. Please hand out the ballots. And gentlemen, as a precaution, I personally checked each ballot. They all have the printed words, 'Eligo in Summum Pontificem' printed plainly on them and nothing else. The paper of the ballot seems perfectly normal."

With that the two elderly gentlemen handed out the ballots and left the Chapel. The only sounds heard were the scratching of pens on paper and some wheezing of the older Cardinals. Then they began the procession to the altar. With the folded ballot held above their head, they again said, "I call as my witness Christ the Lord who will be my judge, that my vote is given to the one who before God I think should be elected." Each Cardinal placed his ballot on the paten and let it slide into the chalice. Again, the ballots from the ailing Cardinals were added to the chalice.

The ritual completed, the three scrutineers stepped forward, and the first poured the ballots into the large urn, counting them as he did so. The number of ballots corresponded to the number of Cardinals present.

"Begin," said Cardinal Perez.

Cardinal Edwardo Gomez reached into the urn and took out a ballot. Hands shaking he opened and read it. Suddenly he wavered unsteadily and then fell back, almost in a faint. The other two scrutineers immediately went to him.

"Cardinal Gomez!" they said in unison.

The second scrutineer, Cardinal Whittier, took the ballot and read it. He immediately seemed flustered and sat on the floor, dropping the ballot. "Oh my God!" he said.

Cardinal Jillison, the third scrutineer picked up the ballot. Racing to the altar, Cardinal Perez grabbed the ballot from the Cardinal. He read it and his face grew ashen.

"What is it?" asked one of the Cardinals.

"I don't understand," Cardinal Perez said. "I don't understand how this can happen again. Look at some more of the ballots. Are they all the same?"

"Yes," said Cardinal Jillison.

"Is it that William fellow again?" someone said from the back of the Chapel.

Cardinal Perez looked upward and said, "Yes. Quickly, look at some more of the ballots."

"They all have William Joseph von Meier III written on them."

Cardinal Reardon from the United States said, "It must mean something. I think the Holy Spirit is in this room."

Cardinal Perez said, "It can't be. I know God doesn't work this way. Someone is tricking us. Someone is making a farce of our Concave. They are making us out to be fools."

Cardinal Signorelli said, "I say again, it's the work of the devil."

"Josip," said the Cardinal from Northern Italy, "It's not the work of the devil. It is a miracle. The Holy Spirit must feel this man can help our Church. We must find him."

"No! No! No!" said Cardinal Perez. "It is a trick. It is someone doing a magic trick. Go back to St. Martha's house and I'll check this out. We'll perform an even more thorough check of the Chapel. We'll vote again tomorrow."

"No. You've checked enough," said Cardinal Turner. Today is the twentieth day. We have to announce a Pope soon. The people are waiting."

"We can't tell the world we've elected some unknown man," said Cardinal Perez. "We'll get laughed off the street. No one here knows this William Joseph von Meier III, do you? Has anyone here heard of him?"

There was no answer.

Cardinal Raymundo said, "Let's all of us call our bishops. Let's see if they ever heard of this man. Surely if he is truly a candidate he must be a bishop or at least a priest somewhere in the world."

"Yes," they agreed.

Cardinal Paulo said, "I still think it is the work of the devil."

"Oh be still, Fredrico. I think it is a miracle," said Cardinal Edwardo Bendino.

"It can't be a miracle," said Cardinal Madelo. "There's no saint involved here."

"I think we should vote one more time," said Cardinal Perez.

"We don't have time to waste. Our people are waiting." someone said.

Cardinal Jillison said, "I know we usually try to disguise our handwriting but let us first sign our name on the ballot and then write our choice."

"Good! Good! That's a great idea," said an excited Cardinal Madelo. "Then we'll see if it is truly the work of the Holy Spirit."

"Let's do it right now," said Cardinal Bendino.

"Call the Masters of Ceremonies back. Have them give out some more ballots again," said Cardinal Perez. "Brethren, you will write your name under the *Eligo in Summum Pontificem*."

The two elder Masters of Ceremonies were called back into the Chapel, somewhat confused. "What is happening?" they said.

Briskly, Cardinal Perez said, "Just hand out some ballots."

"I didn't see any smoke," one of the elders said. "It's almost four."

"What about dinner?" said Cardinal Rezinsky.

"Forget about food, Earl." Then to the elders, "Just hand out the ballots and leave."

The two men handed out 116 ballots and left the room. For the third time they took two ballots to the ill Cardinals, Cardinal Garcia and Cardinal McNiff. Once again the doors were locked and the Cardinals sat down and began voting. This time there was no discussing their choices. They just began to write.

Cardinal McMillan said, "I can't do this many more times. I am not well."

"Just write your choice - after you sign your name," said Cardinal Perez.

"I know you like to follow custom Josip, "said a Cardinal from the rear of the room, "but can't we hold our Conclave in a bigger and cooler room?"

Cardinal Perez ignored him.

Once again the only noise heard were the pens scratching on paper, and the wheezing of the old Cardinals. And again they processed up to the altar and deposited their ballots into the chalice. The scrutineers then placed them into the urn. The heat was even more oppressive.

Carefully, almost fearfully, the first scrutineer took one of the ballots, unfolded it and read it. This time Cardinal Peligrini, a third replacement scrutineer read again and gave it the second scrutineer, Cardinal McKernon. The two scrutineers showed no emotion. They then handed it to the third scrutineer Cardinal Arrasenti.

With no hesitation he said out loud, "Cardinal Gomez, you have written William Joseph von Meier III.

"With God as my witness, I have not written that name!" said Cardinal Gomez.

"Here it is. Look at it." Cardinal Arrasenti handed it to the Cardinal.

"This is my signature but I swear I did not write that man's name!"

Cardinal Perez said, "Get another ballot."

The scrutineer took another ballot. He read it out loud. "Cardinal Johnson, you have voted for William Joseph von Meier III."

"This is preposterous, I definitely did not!" he said.

Several Cardinals left their seats and kneeled. "Get on your knees and bow your head. The Holy Spirit is here. He is in this Chapel," they said almost in unison.

Cardinal Perez almost screamed, "God doesn't work this way!"

"You said that before," said Cardinal Pfeiffer. "but I am beginning to wonder about this whole voting procedure. We are losing active Church members. We're not gaining enough new priests, nuns and brothers. Could it be this man can do something none of us could do in the past? Maybe this bishop or priest can revitalize our Church with a new method to increase religious vocations."

"Then why doesn't Jesus just come into this room and tell us who to elect?" said Cardinal Perez. "Why doesn't he just appear like He did when the apostles were locked in the room in fear after Christ was crucified? Christ just suddenly appeared to them even though the doors were locked."

"Maybe He's doing it," said Cardinal Pfeiffer. "I've just read some statistics. Listen to this. In 1981 the ratio of Catholics to priests was 875 to 1. In 2012 the ratio was 2,000 to 1. I got these notes from the *America Magazine*.

"Don't be ridiculous. Do you think God is doing this election farce just to increase our priestly population? He doesn't work that way."

"How many times are you going to say that, Josip?" said Cardinal Signorelli. "How do you know God doesn't work that way?"

Cardinal Perez bowed his head. In almost a murmur he said again, "God doesn't work that way."

"I know you're disappointed, Josip," said Cardinal Whittier. "You thought you had it sewed up, didn't you?"

Cardinal Johnson said, "What color smoke should I send up?"

"Black."

"No," said Cardinal Paulo.

"What?" said Cardinal Perez.

"I said no. There is no need. We have been told who to elect, directly from God."

"God doesn't work..."

"Be still, Josip. I don't want to hear that again. Do we truly know how God works?"

The next most senior Cardinal Michael Charlo, said, "We'll take a vote on what to do next. I say we should call all of our bishops and see if any of them know of this priest."

Almost unanimously they agreed, except for Cardinal Randondi and a few others. Cardinal Randoni said, "I still think it is some kind of magic trick. I say we should go to a different room. If someone is playing a trick on us, they won't have time to set up their theatrics in a room we randomly pick."

Cardinal Perez's mood suddenly brightened. "Yes, that is an even better idea. We'll go to the Church of Santo Stefano. I'll have the Guards remove any visitors and arrange transportation. Remember, no words to anyone."

Even though it was getting late in the afternoon, in an unprecedented move, the Conclave moved to a new location. The public's curiosity was on the verge of hysteria. The 118 Cardinals including the ill Cardinals were transported to the Church of Santo Stefano. They were hastily seated in some order and an urn was set up to receive their ballots. Two guards were chosen at random to hand out the ballots and pens. The Cardinals were instructed to again write their name on their ballot and then write their choice for Pope. The ballots were placed in an urn just as before.

Cardinal Paulo said, "How will we show our results? There is no stove here to create smoke."

"Don't worry about it, Fredrico," said Cardinal Perez. "We'll just announce it."

Nervously a scrutineer reached into the urn and unfolded the ballot. With an exasperated sigh he threw down his hands and said, "It's no use. God the Holy Spirit is demanding we elect William Joseph von Meier III."

Cardinal Cesario slowly walked up to the altar and randomly opened several more ballots. "Yes, it is true. I feel God has spoken again. I don't like it but what else can we do?'

"I'm not going to accept this vote," said Cardinal Giovani Signorelli. "It's entirely wrong."

"You have no choice. We will have to find this man." All the Cardinals present agreed. "We have to admit, however it was accomplished, we have a majority."

Cardinal Signorelli angrily shouted, "We have a majority, true, but we didn't vote the majority. It was done by some trick. The ballots show a majority on paper but it wasn't our vote. We didn't write that name and it looks like my signature but I didn't vote for that man."

Cardinal Stanlove said, "I agree."

"The Holy Spirit wrote that name," said Cardinal Cesario.

"It's a farce. I will go to my grave swearing I didn't vote for this man."

Cardinal Menzotti said, "It seems to me, Giovani, you had eyes on the Papal Throne too."

Cardinals Signorelli and Stanlove indignantly left the room. "We're going to have dinner."

"I'll join you," said Cardinal Rezinsky.

"What color smoke do you gentlemen agree we should send forth?" asked a Cardinal.

"White. Go over to the Sistine Chapel and use the chemicals for white, but I think we should not mention the name as of yet. Cardinal Rezinsky, just burn our notes, not the ballots," said Cardinal Perez. "I think I want to examine them more closely. If you need more paper to create smoke, use some of the unused ballots."

Cardinal Perez gathered the ballots and placed them back into the urn. Taking the urn, he said, "Let's go meet the press. We'll tell them we have a necessary majority vote but we have to contact the man and see if he accepts.It seems to be an outsider; someone outside the Conclave of Cardinals has been chosen,"

"Do you think the public will accept our explanation?" asked a young Cardinal.

"They have no choice."

Cardinal Reardon said, "This is truly a miracle of the Holy Spirit."

In a raised voice Cardinal Perez said, "Stop using the word miracle."

"What word would you like, Josip?"

"Phenomenon."

Tuesday morning there was a flurry of communications to all bishops throughout the world. 118 Cardinals began feverishly calling their home countries, cities and parishes. At this time the older, non-voting Cardinals were not told the reason for the delay in naming a Pope. They thought it would be too confusing and embarrassing. Due to the Cardinals moving from one building to another, the public was aware a serious problem had arisen. Most of the Cardinals were from outside of Rome and desired to return home but Cardinal Camerlengo demanded they remain until the quandary was settled.

The Cardinals' question was the same, "Do you have in your parishes or know of a priest or bishop going by the name of William Joseph von Meier III? Check as quickly as you can and get back to us. Also we'd like to ask that you don't make too big of commotion about it."

And invariably the questions back to the Cardinals were, "Is he to be the next Pope?" And the answer to the question, given with as much ambiguity as possible is, "We need to speak to him as he may have information regarding the next Pope."

After four days of the Roman Catholic World being in a state of uncertainty, no definite name came up. A few William von Meier showed up, but Baptismal Records displayed a different middle name.

"Josip, what now?" asked Cardinal Witter. "This is getting desperate. Do we dare try laymen?"

"That's our only remaining choice. After all, the Pope doesn't have to be a priest or bishop at the time of election. He just has to be a man and a practicing Catholic. Hopefully he can speak Italian but with a name like von Meier III, he surely isn't Italian."

"Okay, send out the message. Find any man with the name of William Joseph von Meier III."

Once again a flurry of communications was dispatched. And once again, no confirmed results. Cardinal Perez stood before a picture of St. Peter. Raising his eyes, he said, "St. Peter. We need help down here. Maybe you and the Holy Spirit can perform another miracle. Our flock is wandering in disarray."

While giving the appearance of trying to find the man named on the ballots, Cardinal Perez had no intention of relinquishing his quest to become Pope.

CHAPTER THREE

David Meier rushed home from Saturday afternoon Mass. His home was a single family, split-level house, a fading white with grey trim, immediately across the street from St. Sabina Church. He was one of the altar servers who served regularly for the church. Since he lived across the street from the church he, and his brother Charles, were frequently called when last minute replacement servers were needed for Mass. This is what happened this afternoon. His parents had attended Saturday afternoon Mass, too. His brother would serve Sunday.

"Dad," he said. "I heard something strange today after Mass."

"And what might that be?" said his tall, distinguished looking father. Bill Meier was a Peoria, Illinois police officer and at six foot, four inches he was an imposing figure. Weighing 240 pounds and all muscle, he was able to defuse many dangerous situations without having to apply force. He had blond hair and blue eyes and a very engaging smile. Bill was a member of the St. Sabina parish council and involved himself in many other parish activities. Currently he was leading the Bible study sessions for parishioners. Bill's fair complexion contrasted sharply to his son's dark eyes and black hair. Bill was 51 years old and David, at fifteen years old, was the second of two children. David's dark appearance took after Rosalie, his Italian mother. He was not as tall as his father but he was well built and definitely still growing. He wanted to play for his school football team but Bill said an emphatic no. He had seen too many of his fellow police officers with reoccurring knee problems from school football injuries. He then tried out for baseball and soccer. David performed well in both. Charles, his brother, was built more like his father and also of fair skin. He hoped he was still growing, having already passed his father's height. He loved baseball but felt he was too tall to play soccer like his brother. Bill did not allow Charles to play football either.

Bill was born in Germany and Rosalie, his wife, was born in Italy. They met in Southern Germany where after several months of long distance dating, they were married.Since Bill spoke German and Rosalie spoke Italian, they had to converse in their limited knowledge of English. They came to the United States for their honeymoon. Their parents were deceased and they had no siblings, so they returned to the United States two years later and stayed.

"I was leaving the vestibule and I overheard Father Johnston talking on the phone. He was telling someone about looking for a man named William Joseph von Meier III. Didn't you say your name was von Meier the third or fourth before you and Mom came to the United States?"

"Yeah," he said. "We dropped the von in von Meier, and the third also. We had it legally changed to Meier to sound a little more American."

"Father Johnston sounded really concerned about it, saying they have to find this man quickly."

Bill said, "I'm sure it's no one related to me."

"Yeah, but Dad, your middle name is Joseph. That's the middle name of the guy they're looking for."

Rosalie came into the room. "What are you guys talking about? Whose middle name?" Rosalie showed her Italian descent by her dark features. Her hair was coal black with streaks of silver showing. Keeping three large men fed kept her busy in the kitchen but she enjoyed preparing Italian meals. Rosalie did fear her fine cooking was beginning to show on her short frame. A foot shorter than Bill, they made a charming couple. She was eagerly looking forward to grandchildren. With college still ahead for her sons, she was willing to wait.

"I was telling Dad, Father Johnston was talking to someone at the Vatican. They are looking for a man named William Joseph von Meier III."

"He was talking to someone in Rome?" she said. "It's the middle of the night there. What in the world for?" she jokingly said. "Maybe they want your Dad to be Pope. They haven't named one yet."

Bill said, "I'm sure the guy has to be a bishop or Cardinal or at least a priest."

"I don't think so," said Rosalie. "He just has to be a Catholic man. Some of the early Popes were even married."

"No kidding," said David. He went to answer the ringing cell phone. "Hello," he said. "Dad, it's for you."

Bill took the phone. "Yes," he said. "Oh, hello, Father Johnston."

David jumped up. "Mom! It's Father Johnston. I bet he wants Dad to be Pope!"

Rosalie started laughing. "I bet. That would make me a Popess, or First Popess."

"Yes Father, I can get them now and bring them over. They are only copies, though. You want me to come to your office with them right now?"

"Charlie," David yelled to his eighteen year old brother. "Dad's going to be Pope!"

"David," said his mother. "Don't start that."

Bill walked back into the room.

"Father Johnston wants me to come over to his office - with my birth certificate, legal name change papers and my Baptismal Record. I told him they are in our safe deposit box but the bank is closed but I have unofficial copies here at home."

"How did he know that your name was von Meier III?" asked Rosalie.

"He heard David tell his buddy Sammy our original name was von Meier."

David sat up. "Gosh, Dad, did I do something wrong?"

"No, I'm sure it's just some kind of mix up. I'm sure over in Germany there's some guy or some bishop or a priest named von Meier III."

"Bill," said Rosalie, "This is weird. It's scary."

"I'm good but not good enough to be Pope," said Bill flippantly hoping nothing would come of this.

"That's true, Bill. You're a good man, a good husband, good provider and a good father. And even if that is all you'll ever be that's enough for me."

"I feel I should pray to God but I don't know what to pray for."

Rosalie said, "Just go see Father and come home for dinner. You took the weekend off to work on the bathroom remodel. It's almost six. Come home and we'll bar-be-que something."

"Yeah," came a half-hearted response from Bill.

Charles ran into the room. "What's going on? Dad's going to be Pope?"

No, no," said Rosalie. "It seems they are looking for a priest or bishop with the same name as your father."

"Man, wouldn't that be something? You know, Dave? Soccer's big in Europe. We could easily get on an Italian team."

Rosalie said, "Would you boys stop it? You're being ridiculous."

Bill entered St. Sabina Church through the side entrance. The secretary Mary saw him and immediately went to him. She looked at Bill through rimless glasses, "Bill, come in. Father wants to see you right away."

"Okay," said Bill scratching his blond hair.

Father Johnston almost ran to see him. "Bill, Bill, come on in," he said. The priest was a short man with balding, red hair and a large waist. Although he never player sports, he was an enthusiastic Chicago Cubs fan and he and Bill discussed the team's difficulties quite often.

"Sit down," said the priest.

Late afternoon sun filtered in through faded curtains. Bill looked around as classical music quietly filled the room. He sat down in a comfortable grey, leather chair. On an end table next to his chair was a picture of the Sacred Heart of Jesus. It was one of those three dimensional pictures where the eyes follow you around the room. There were several shelves full of religious books and brochures. A thick burgundy carpet covered the floor. He noted several plants in the room, some in desperate need of water. The walls were covered with many pictures of Popes including the Pope recently deceased.

"Do you have your records?"

"Oh. Yeah, I got them," he said. "Like I said, they are not the official records. Father, you've got to explain to me what this is about. Is it about my name? I have completely lost track of all my ancestors. Are the Cardinals looking for a von Meier III?"

Father Johnston sat down behind a well-worn but polished oak desk. "I have here a communication from our Cardinal Peter Whittier. It came to me by way of our Bishop. It states that the Cardinals have elected, by some strange means, a William Joseph von Meier III. They are having problems locating this man. All bishops are instructed to help find this man. He..., ah..., is, ah, supposed to be our next Pope. It is extremely urgent we find this man."

Bill said, "But what's that got to do with me? I happen to have the same name as some other guy but it's not me."

Ignoring Bill's question, Father Johnston said, "Let me see your Baptismal record, birth certificate and legal name change."

Bill was slightly bewildered by what seemed to be happening. Father Johnston did not appear to be listening and this worried him. He gave the impression he was only concerned with Bill's records, examining them closely.

"They're not official," said Bill again.

"All your papers seem to be in order. We'll check the originals later." he said. "You were baptized in Germany. You were confirmed, too, weren't you? "

"Yes."

"And married in the Church?"

"Yes. Father, you have to let me know what is happening?" said Bill. "At first Rosalie and I laughed it off as some kind of mistake. Now I'm a little scared. Should I be?"

"Bill, William," said Father Johnston, "We are having quite a problem, or should I say, the Conclave in Rome is having a problem. I might as well let you have the complete story. The name of William Joseph von Meier III appeared on all the ballots each of the four times the Cardinals voted. Yet, not one of the Cardinals had written your name. They cannot explain it. Some say it is a miracle by the Holy Spirit and some don't know what to say."

Bill sat speechless.

"The one thing we are sure of, Bill," said Father Johnston, "is that it is not some trick manufactured by you. I don't think you'd ever arrange to have someone do this kind of trick. But, as to how it happened we just don't know. I have to now call the Vatican to see our next step"

"Father," said Bill. "I don't know what's going on but if this turns out to be true, I don't want to be the Pope. I'm not a good enough Catholic to be Pope. I just might get into heaven by the skin of my teeth, if I get in at all. I hardly even go to confession."

Father Johnston again did not seem to be listening, nodding slightly.

"Bill, do you have a passport?"

"Father, are you listening to me? I don't want to be Pope, I can't be the Pope." Bill stood up to add emphasis to his words.

Father Johnston asked Bill to be seated again. "Bill, if Jesus Christ suddenly appeared in this room and asked you to be Pope, would you refuse?"

"That won't happen," said Bill. "Miracles just don't happen anymore."

Father gave Bill a knowing glance. "I think one just happened; not here, but in Rome, in front of 118 Cardinals."

"I want to go home."

"First, Bill," said Father. "Can you answer my question? Would you refuse Jesus?"

"Father, I'm not a bishop. I'm not a priest. I'm not a good Catholic. I commit sins of all kinds. Probably the only sin I haven't committed is murder. I'm a policeman. I carry a gun. I thank God every day that I've never had to use my pistol to shoot a human being, but there could easily be a day when I'd have to make a decision to kill someone."

Father Johnston looked at Bill, a slight smile on his face. "Bill, have you ever heard the saying, 'God works in mysterious ways'?"

"Come on Father. Do you really think a guy like me could be, should be, a Pope? It's ridiculous."

"I ask you again, would you refuse Jesus? I'll tell you this, Bill," said Father Johnston. "Cardinal Perez has told me to tell you, if you agree, we will furnish plane tickets for you and your wife and get you both quick passports. We'll pay for the tickets and surcharge for quick passports."

"You already told the guys in Rome about me? Wait a minute. I didn't agree to this yet."

'Like I said, Bill. There's a bit of a rush. Go home and talk it over with Rosalie. It'll take up to three days to get the passports. I think God is calling you, Bill. I see you doing something around the church here several times a week. He must feel you are needed in the Church. There must be something about you that He likes. Can Charlie and David take care of things at home?"

"Yes, but..."

Father Johnston looked at his calendar. "We don't have much time. Go home and discuss it with Rosalie. Both of you can then come down here tomorrow afternoon and we'll talk some more about this. Quite honestly, Cardinal Whittier, Bishop Cartwright and I are very excited about this. Just think, the Pope came from Peoria, Illinois. From my parish. The Pope from Peoria. Wow."

"Father, this is stupid. It's ridiculous. They are flying me to Rome on a whim. A magic trick."

"This is not on a whim, Bill. They want to see you in person and interview you. Think about it. Pray about it. You and Rosalie come in tomorrow and we'll talk some more. Even though Cardinal Perez is probably asleep, I have been told to contact him immediately and tell him of our progress. We should have your tickets and passports by Friday."

As Bill left the priest's office, Mary stood up. "Oh Bill," said Mary. "I can't believe it. It's marvelous."

"You heard?"

"I couldn't help it," she said. "When Father told me to make the call to the Bishop I couldn't believe it. Father Johnston set up a conference call to Rome with our Bishop Cartwright and some Cardinal in the Vatican. Due to the time zone change I think I woke up the Cardinal but the Bishop had a special number to call immediately if we found our man. And we did!"

Bill stuck his head back in Father Johnston's office and said, "Am I the only William Joseph von Meier III they have located?"

"So far, Bill," said Father. "They're so sure they are arranging plane fare for you and Rosalie."

William Joseph von Meier III walked home in a daze wondering what if what Father said was true. Why did God pick me?

CHAPTER FOUR

After a week of confusion, Cardinal Perez called several Cardinals in his office. "Well, gentlemen, we seem to have found a man with the name appearing on our ballots – and he seems to be the only man we've located with the name William Joseph von Meier III. Another man was located but he couldn't verify the 'third'. The man we've located lives in the United States, in the state of Illinois. He is a policeman in the city of Peoria. His parish priest Father Johnston, said he is a Catholic in good standing. He's on the parish council, he moderates a Bible Study meeting for adults and he volunteers for other committees. He's married with two boys, ages fifteen and eighteen."

"A policeman," said Cardinal Peligrini. "You can't be serious."

"Yes, I am serious. I have already had plane tickets arranged for him and his wife. They should have their passports by now."

Cardinal Jillison said, "This is becoming a nightmare. Do you feel he is the William Joseph von Meier III we are searching for?"

"I do for now," said Cardinal Perez.

Cardinal Reardon said, "Do you think we should look outside of our dioceses?" You know, non-Catholics?"

"No, if he's not a Catholic, I don't want him. This William is a practicing Catholic in good standing in his parish. It does make me wonder what God has in mind. A policeman Pope, how unusual."

"Don't be frivolous, Josip."

Cardinal Perez had a wiry smile. "Can you imagine the contrast to previous Popes? Most have been quite old and stooped shouldered. Father Johnston said he is a large, tall, well-built man. Can you envision the world seeing a strapping young man as our Pope?"

"How old is he?"

"Fifty one," said Cardinal Josip. "That's young as Popes go."

"This isn't becoming a nightmare, said Cardinal Jillison, "it already is one."

Cardinal Perez stood up with a wily smile. "Gentlemen, you all know I had the wish to become Pope but I think this is even more interesting. Just think. If God, or the Holy Spirit, has directly intervened, this could be something tremendously important to our faith. It's been many, many years since a direct or unquestionably obvious miracle, or I prefer the word incident, has happened in our history. In the past several centuries all miracles performed by saints have been dismissed by non-believers as coincidences. The non-believers could be correct, they could be coincidences but they can't argue with this incident."

"You're forgetting Mother Teresa," said Cardinal Jillison.

Cardinal Perez said, "Don't be argumentative. Also gentlemen, for your information I've presented an *Actor Causae* to the Theologians of the Congregation for the Causes of Saints. They said they were not interested at this time. As we said earlier, there is no person being considered for sainthood."

Cardinal Di Magio said, "Josip, do you realize this man could wreck the Church? He would become a loose cannon. Down through the ages the Church has corrected its many faults. We are just now getting close to perfection."

"Andrew," said Cardinal Mc Kernon, "are you saying we are close to perfection?"

"No, but... yes. I am saying we are close to perfection."

"Ridiculous," said Cardinal Randondi. "Look how we are losing members. Look at the problem we are having getting new priests and nuns. Look how we are even losing the priests, nuns and brothers we have.And look how we are losing active Catholics. Any man, or woman, putting on a collar backwards can draw a congregation better than we can. Look at the sexual problems we're having. I feel sometimes we're becoming to be known as a haven for gays and lesbians."

"He's right, look at the scandals we are having." said Cardinal Rezinsky. "You can rent an auditorium, add a bunch of folding chairs, hire a youthful five piece band and colorful banners and you got a congregation. And if the reverend is an energetic, vibrant orator, you've got a formidable church."

Cardinal Flanis said, "In the States I am always amazed at how full the parking lots are at these churches. And," he added with emphasis, "they don't leave early!"

Cardinal Perez stood up before the group. "Gentleman, this man is on his way here, or will soon be. I think we will have to interview him as a group and then individually. I know the public is waiting but he has to get his passport. All we can do is wait. Unless he turns out to be an evil man, or another William Joseph von Meier III shows up, he'll be appointed as our next Pope. God help us."

Despite words to the contrary, Cardinal Perez had not given up his desire to be pope, by any means. Back in his office he began looking up detective agencies.

CHAPTER FIVE

William and Rosalie sat nervously in their first class seats. It seemed as if they had spent the entire Sunday in an airplane. After waiting a week for their passports the uneasy couple was on their way to Rome. They had attended Saturday afternoon Mass yesterday and Father Johnston could not hold back his enthusiasm regarding his parishioner possibly being the next pope. Father, and his secretary, had to take an oath of secrecy to tell no one of Bill's trip to Rome. Father Johnston also told William no other William von Meier III had been found.

The flight attendant asked if there was anything they wanted.

"No thanks," said Bill. "Rosalie, I think it's been almost thirty years since we left Italy."

"Yes, it has," said Rosalie in a weak voice. "Bill, I'm sick. I don't understand what's happening. This is becoming a nightmare."

"Just relax, dear. Let's just enjoy our trip to Italy. I'm sure they'll find the real Pope, or Pope elect. There's no way I'll be a Pope. The Catholic Church would collapse in ruin if I became Pope. God won't let it happen. Be realistic. Just think. Bill Meier; a Pope? Jesus Christ Himself would have to come down to Earth again to straighten things out if I became pope. Just enjoy the trip. I've never flown first class. This is great."

"Oh, Bill," was all Rosalie could say.

"This is really interesting stuff about the Popes and the Vatican. I always wondered how the leaders of our Church got from Jerusalem to Rome. It was Peter who moved it there. I guess he felt more comfortable in Rome."

Rosalie said, "What are you reading? Why didn't you bring your Kindle?"

"Too much trouble and the library is free. I got these books from the library before we left. According to what I've read, we have had quite an assortment of Popes. Some were downright bad with mistresses and others just plain corrupt. There was even a time in our early Church history when there were two Popes at the same time. I read about rumors of a woman pope, although she hid her gender. Some were married with legitimate children and even illegitimate children. If the man elected pope was married, it was demanded of him to cease having intercourse with his wife. Some early Popes weren't even bishops or priests. If we have access to the internet, I'm going to Google more current stuff."

Rosalie said, "I wonder what the library will think about you taking their books to Rome."

"They won't care as long as I get them back by the due date."

The flight attendant announced their arrival in Rome in 30 minutes.

As Bill and his wife entered the reception area of Leonardo De Vinci airport, terminal C, Bill said,"They told me to look for a person holding a *Welcome home, Joseph* sign. They didn't want to attract any more attention than necessary. It seems the word has got out. I'm supposed to walk down the concourse with this St. Louis Cardinal's flight bag prominently displayed. How appropriate."

The exhausted couple spotted their man with the sign. He was a large man wearing a dark suit, white shirt, black tie and dark glasses.

"Gosh," said Bill. "He looks like a secret service man."

"Mr. William von Meier? Over here," said the man in a heavily Italian accent. "I'm Anthony Rossi. Our vehicle is this way. Welcome to Italy."

They were quickly ushered through customs and immigration and escorted to a black limousine.

"Your luggage is being picked up by Vito."

"How will he get it through customs?" asked Bill.

"Don't worry, he'll get it," said Anthony.

As Bill and Rosalie climbed into the limo, they heard their luggage being heaved into the trunk of the car. Anthony and Vito got in the limo and began their winding trip through the streets of Rome.

"Where are we going?" asked Bill.

"To Torre San Giovanni," said Anthony. "This is where most guests of the Vatican are housed."

"What?"

"The Tower of St. John."

"Oh. Is that where the Pope lives?" asked Rosalie.

"Hardly."

Bill asked Rosalie, "You were never in Rome while you lived in Italy, were you?"

"No. We couldn't afford to travel much."

Bill said, "My parents brought me to Rome once when I was quite young. I don't remember much of it. It seemed like an awfully long trip from Cologne."

Bill asked Vito, "Will we get to tour much of Rome and the Vatican before we head back home?"

"Head back home? What do you mean? I believe this is your new home and you'll get a nice tour soon."

Bill sat up in his seat, "Oh no. This is a big mistake. We just wanted to see Rome. It was a selfish reason but we hadn't been back to Europe for thirty years. I guarantee you in a week we'll be winging our way back to the USA."

"I know there will be a ton of laundry to do with Charles and David living alone," said Rosalie. "The house will be a mess."

Bill said, "Don't worry. I gave the boys clear instructions before we left and Martha said she'd check on them every day. From next door she can watch for any wild parties. Can't you just relax and enjoy the sights?"

"No," said Rosalie.

The driver took them to a building along a wall. "This wall was built by Pope Nicholas III, "said Anthony. Entering the gates to Vatican City, they saw many tourists milling around.

"I don't see any cars," said Rosalie.

In his deep voice, Anthony said, "No public automobiles are allowed in the Vatican unless they are here on official business."

"Oh." Rosalie thought as they drove into St. Peter's Square. We must be official business.

Anthony ushered the wearied couple to their room. "This is where you'll stay for the time being. It's been many years – or should I say – centuries since a woman lived in the Pope's quarters. They had to bring some nuns over to help with arrangements."

"I hope they don't go to too much trouble for our short stay here," said Rosalie.

"Mrs. Meier," said Anthony. "I don't think you understand. Pope is for life, unless he retires. Your husband is quite young. You could be here for quite a few years."

Rosalie did not answer and just walked to a window. She thought, what if they ask me to divorce Bill.

As Vito placed their luggage in the room he said, "They told me they'll give you a day or two to get used to the time change. You are free to walk about the grounds if you wish but wear these badges around your neck since no one will recognize you at this time. The first building you see over there is the Marconi Radio Transmission Center. It was established by Guglielmo Marconi in 1931 for Pope Pius XI. Here is a map of the grounds. Cardinal Perez wants to meet you as soon as possible tomorrow but he'll call first. I would wait, Mrs. von Meier, to visit the museums. It'll be much more enjoyable if a staff member escorts you. Feel free to go wherever you'd like. The badges will let you in anywhere."

"Relax," said Anthony. "No one will call on you today except in time for meals. With the time change you may not know you are hungry. There are no public restaurants on Vatican grounds but employees, staff and clergy can eat at the cafeteria. The food is quite good. There are, however, several restaurants right outside the Vatican gates – and several pizza restaurants. Our pizza is a little different than yours in the states I'm told. Oh, it's four o'clock local time."

"Bill," asked Rosalie. "How much time did you ask off from the department?"

"A week."

"It worries me that they didn't give us our return air tickets."

Anthony stood at the door. "Don't worry. They will give you transportation and time to close your affairs back in the States."

"Bill," said Rosalie in a louder than usual voice. "I want to go home!"

"I do too. Don't worry, dear. I'm not going to be Pope. I've always wanted to tour the Vatican, and Rome. This is a great chance and it won't cost us a penny. I did a lot of reading on the plane about this Pope thing and I can simply refuse."

"You promise?"

"Yes. I can't wait to tell the guys at the station about this."

Anthony shook his head and closed the door. The bewildered couple sat on the bed in silence.

"They sure could have given us better furnishings," said Rosalie. "I don't like bare walls and high ceilings. I bet they will want us to get a divorce."

"I told you there's been married Popes," said Bill

"Not lately."

"You should read what they did to the early Pope's children, legitimate and illegitimate."

Rosalie sighed, "I don't think I want to. I'm afraid I am becoming disenchanted with our faith."

"Don't. For centuries Catholicism has been trying to improve. Hey! Maybe God wants me to help."

"William, don't be frivolous.

CHAPTER SIX

Cardinal Perez sat in front of 118 Cardinals, the two ill Cardinals were brought to the gathering in wheel chairs. He began the meeting with a prayer. "My brethren, Mr. William von Meier III and his wife arrived in Rome yesterday afternoon. I had them informed we will give them a day to get acclimated. We will meet with William Tuesday. We have quite a formidable task ahead of us. We have to decide how to approach this dilemma. As we all have said many times; is this message from God, a message from Satan, some trick by a prankster or simply a fluke. With that in mind we have to decide what questions to ask of this man. His parish priest, Father Johnston, assured me this man is not the kind to pull a stunt like this. He sincerely doubts William desires to be Pope. It reminds me of the conversion of St. Paul. He was a soldier and was allegedly struck down and asked by God, 'Why do you persecute me?' I think we should interview him collectively and then, if anyone desires, individually. What do you think?"

All the Cardinals agreed. Cardinal Santo spoke up, "What about his wife? Should she be present during our interview?"

"Not at first," said Cardinal Perez. "We'll interview her later."

Cardinal Signorelli spoke up. "You can't be serious. Are we going to seriously consider this man? We could be going back to the third century. I'm sure you can remember in your studies of the early Church, the turmoil it went through. This man – a policeman - probably thinks Canon Law refers to rules of artillery warfare."

"His parish priest, Father Johnston, assured me he is an intelligent man. He was an Air Policeman in the United States Air Force and then attended a community college in his home town studying law enforcement. That says a lot about a man who became a United States citizen."

"So I guess no matter what we'll have to interrogate him," said Cardinal Stanlove.

"Let's call it an interview. He's not a criminal," said Cardinal Whittier. Cardinal Whittier was assigned to Chicago three years ago. He was an energetic man of sixty years of age and was known as a liberal thinking cardinal. He was conversant in several languages especially Italian. His slight stature of five feet, six inches gave the appearance of a timid man but he was far from being inhibited. He was quite vocal in Church affairs, sometimes irritating more conservative cardinals.

"Is that because he is from your home state of Illinois?" said Cardinal Perez.

The Cardinal just smiled.

"Whatever. Anyway, we have to do it immediately. We don't want our food cut off." Cardinal Rezinsky was referring to another of the early Church's practice to hasten the choosing of a Pope. Food to the Sistine Chapel was reduced slightly each day as an inducement for a quick decision.

'Earl," said Cardinal Perez, "you would be the one to think about food."

Cardinal Rezinsky looked away.

"It's agreed then. Tomorrow morning after prayers we'll meet with this William Meier in the Sistine Chapel. Let's hope the Holy Spirit is still around to guide us."

Cardinal Signorelli said, "I want to go on record as being vehemently against this farce. I will fight this vote. This man will never be Pope."

"I concur," said Cardinal Stanlove.

"I don't see any way this man can be pope, no matter how good a Catholic he is," said Cardinal Perez.

CHAPTER SEVEN

The Tuesday meeting was postponed until Wednesday, about 40 hours since their arrival in Rome. The couple appreciated the extra day to get acclimated. They had casually walked around some of the Vatican grounds but not too far from their apartment. Bill and Rosalie were very intimidated with the vastness of the buildings.

There was a knock on the door of Bill and Rosalie's room. Bill answered it. "Good morning," said a young priest. "I'm Father John Thiel and this is Sister Rose Williams. I'm to take you, William, to meet the Cardinals and Sister will take Mrs. Meier on a tour of the Vatican."

By his accent Father Thiel was evidently of German descent. He had long blond hair, clean shaven and clear, blue eyes. He was six feet, three inches, almost the same height as William. The priest was a broad shouldered man, thirty years of age and looking forward to his first assignment at a parish hopefully in Germany. Sister Rose William was of Hispanic descent about thirty five, five feet seven. She was slender with a dark complexion and quite bubbly of nature.

He said, "We have several shuttles for transportation."

"Oh, can't I go with Bill?" said Rosalie.

Father said, "For now, the Cardinals want to interview William alone. Later they will see both of you. You'll have dinner together tonight, probably lunch, too."

Bill climbed into his little shuttle and Rosalie got into hers. They zipped off in opposite directions.

"Where are we going?" asked Bill.

"The Cardinals decided to meet you in the Sistine Chapel," said Father Thiel. "I guess you can say that's where it all began."

"You can say that again," said Bill.

"They told me you were born in Germany. I was born in Mainz, just south of Cologne. I guess that's why they picked me to escort you around."

Bill looked uneasily at Father Thiel. "Father, I don't want to appear rude but I can't be Pope. This has to be some sort of mistake."

"I don't understand all that's happening either but the Cardinals have elected you and of course, you could always refuse."

"I will have to refuse or God will send me directly to Hell."

Father Thiel laughed heartily. "I'll say one thing. You're a modest man. And you'll be the first Pope taller and more athletic than I."

"I'm also missing my morning workout."

Father Thiel smiled again, "We have complete gym facilities here. The Swiss Guards work out there daily. They have quite a routine since 1981 when Pope John Paul II was attacked."

"Yeah, I remember that."

"Okay. Here we are."

"I have no idea where I am," said Bill

Father Thiel handed him a map. "Here's what we give to tourists." Pointing to the map he said, "Here's where you were and here's where you are."

"Great."

A Cardinal in black with a red sash around his waists and red cap was standing at the door.

Father said, "See you later."

"I'm sure you'll be taking us to the airport."

"Like I said, Mr. Meier, you're so modest. And please call me John."

William climbed out of the little vehicle. The Cardinal approached him with an outstretched hand.

"Good morning, William. I'm Cardinal Cesario but since you'll soon be our leader you can call me Juan. We're not really so formal. Did you and your wife sleep well?"

The words, 'You'll soon be our leader,' took Bill by surprise. "Ah... yes. We slept well. It wasn't that hard to get used to the time change."

"Come in," said the Cardinal.

Bill was surprised how small the Sistine Chapel was. There were quite a few Cardinals sitting around long tables. He also expected them to be dressed in flowing red vestments. They were all wearing black vestment type outfits with white collars around their neck and red waist sash and cap. He had read that the usual colors were white for the Pope, red for Cardinals, purple for bishops and black for priests. Father Thiel told William there should be more than 100 Cardinals present. Even the Cardinals too ill to attend the voting were present. They said this time they would not miss this for the world. Some of the Cardinals rose as William walked in – and some did not. He was escorted to the front of the Chapel. This was Bill's most nervous moment since Father Johnston's phone call. The room was fairly warm, and small, making Bill sweat even more.

Cardinal Perez stood up. "Mr. William Joseph von Meier III. Is that your full birth and Baptized name?"

"Yes, your ah...honor. I'm sorry. I don't know how to address you sir." Bill was slightly amused by the Cardinal's halting English with the Spanish accent.

Cardinal Perez stood erect emphasizing his five feet, six inches and said. "You will address me as Cardinal Perez."

"Your Eminence will suffice," said Cardinal Marshall. "Later you may call us by our first name."

Cardinal Perez glared at the Cardinal.

Cardinal Perez looked back at William. "As you have probably guessed, we are perplexed as to how your name appeared on our ballots. Do you have any idea?"

"No. I do not," said Bill.

"Some of us here believe it is the work of the Holy Spirit, some of us believe it is the work of Satan, some of us believe it is the work of some trickster or magician and some of us don't know what to believe. What do you believe?"

"Your Eminence, I think it is some kind of mistake. I can no more be Pope than Hitler – and I use his name since I am of German descent. I am not trying to be flippant."

An Italian Cardinal at the rear of the room said, "What does flippant mean?"

"Careless, as a smart aleck, and please learn some of these American slang words, Antonio," said Cardinal Perez. "William just may be our next Pope."

Cardinal Perez continued, "I can say this much, Mr. von Meier– or Mr. Meier as you prefer–in speaking with your Pastor Father Johnston we do not believe this is any kind of trick you have concocted. But I am here to say, I will find out how this happened and why. I have contacted a very well-known and successful private detective, Mr. Edwardo Candelo. He has a very efficient staff in the United States and other countries as well as here in Italy. He will meet with me soon and he'll have an answer quickly."

"Who is paying for this great detective, Josip?" said Cardinal Di Maggio.

Cardinal Josip Perez ignored the questions. He began pacing across the front of the Chapel.

"What do you think of the Catholic Church?" he said.

"What do you mean?" Bill said. "I don't think about the Church much at all. I go to Mass every Sunday and Holy Days, I tithe, I go to Communion and once in a while I go to Confession. I should add there have been times when duty caused me to miss Sunday Mass. I am on the parish council and I also hold a Biblical education meeting for adults once a month. As for as the Church itself, I know nothing of importance."

"What I mean is, do you think the Church has any flaws?"

Bill looked around at all the Cardinals, black vestments flowing in the man-made breeze of the fans.

"Any business or corporation has flaws. Look at my country, the United States. We're stumbling around with our flaws but we're trying to correct them. I brought several Vatican books from the library to read on the flight over here. From what I have read, in the time from about the two hundredth century to about the nineteenth century, you – or should I say – we have had several bad Popes and many bad decisions handed down. Many of these problems have been corrected and I imagine some more will be corrected in the future. Of course in that span of time we have had many great popes, too."

Cardinal Perez stood straighter, "You mean you think our Church still has flaws?"

"Hell...oops. Heavens yes. Don't you?"

"So, if you were Pope you'd make wholesale changes?" Cardinal Perez's voice getting louder.

Cardinal Marshall, an elder Cardinal, said, "Josip. Would you come here a minute?"

Cardinal Perez glared at the man and then slowly walked over to the old man.

"Yes. What do you want, Harold?"

Whispering he said, "I think you're losing your focus here. If God truly gave us this man's name, there must be a reason. And if he has novel ideas, he may be an answer to our problems."

"Ridiculous."

Cardinal Bendido asked a question of William, "What do you think of abortion?"

"Not having studied all situations, I believe it's murder. Actually from what I briefly read, there is no clear cut answer in the Bible."

"What are you saying?" screamed Cardinal Di Magio.

"It's simply Biblical interpretation," said William.

"What Bible are you reading?" said the Cardinal pounding the table.

Cardinal Whittier jumped into the fray. "Relax, Andrew. William seems to have read the same writings we have read. We all know there is a lot of interpretation by the original writers and by those who translated it from Greek."

Cardinal Di Maggio sat down, still steaming.

"What about priestly celibacy and birth control?" asked Cardinal McMillian.

"I think it's..."

"Hold on!" yelled Cardinal Perez. "I'm conducting this interview. I'll ask the questions."

Cardinal Signorelli said, "Josip. I know you're dead set against this man to be Pope. So am I, but you're not running this meeting. We're all here as equals. Let me ask one simple question."

"Go ahead," said a chastised Cardinal Perez.

"Mr. Meier, do you want to be Pope?"

"No."

"Why not?"

William looked at a Crucifix. "I am not a holy man. As I said before, I have probably committed every sin except murder. I am a policeman. I carry a pistol. I have not had to use it but if I ever had to use it to protect someone, I am sure I would. It is my sworn duty. How could I be a Pope our people would respect? I have had to strong arm bad people to the ground and handcuff them. I am not Pope material as they say. I have shown anger to my wife, sons and fellow officers. As I make my rounds I have been seriously tempted by prostitutes but by the grace of God I haven't fallen. I am just a simple human. I am not saint material. You men are. I just hope my deceased saintly mother will convince Our Blessed Mother to let me in Heaven when I die. I sincerely appreciate allowing my wife and me to visit the Vatican. I appreciate everyone's courtesy. I hate to tell you this but I committed a sin by coming to Rome. I wanted to see the city and allow my wife to see the Vatican at no expense to us. I came here with selfish reasons. I should go to confession before I get on the plane to go home."

"I like him," said Cardinal Paulo.

"Fredrico, you seem to have changed your opinion of a few minutes ago. You've always had odd ideas regarding the Church," said Cardinal Perez. "It seems to me you were calling this the work of the devil."

"No I haven't changed but I'm trying to remain open minded."

"I'll ask the question again, what do you think of priestly celibacy?" asked Cardinal McMillan.

Bill again looked around as if seeking help. "Please don't ask me questions like that. What I have done after I knew I'd be speaking to you was read as much as I could from some library books about the Vatican and a lot more on Google. There's no way..."

An elderly Cardinal interrupted, "What is this Google?"

Cardinal Perez said, "Graco, you should get up to date on the latest internet search engines." To William, Cardinal Perez said, "As you can see, Cardinal Madino doesn't keep up to date on the current internet programs."

"What I was going to say is there's no way I'll be Pope. If you want my opinion, I say priests should be allowed to marry. They did in the early Church and it didn't hurt anything. Actually how could an unmarried priest give sound advice to a troubled marriage never having participated in the sacrament? And if he never raised a child, he would be at a great loss understanding a juvenile's mind. You say it distracts from their mission but brain surgeons or aircraft pilots or world leaders marry with few problems. Well, I guess some marriages have problems."Bill smiled at that thought.

A younger Cardinal Reardon said, "You realize your Google is a lot of facts mixed in with opinions."

"I understand that. I tried to consider the sources and looked at different responses. Also, in my Bible sessions, I've learned a lot. I know quite a few Bible verses, too."

Cardinal DiMagio asked, "What about gays and lesbians?"

"One of my fellow officers is gay. I don't believe in it but I have worked with him. I have no problem with that as long as he doesn't try to convince me it's normal. Some people like Chevrolets and some like Fords. Just don't try to tell me your automobile is better than mine."

"Interesting," said the Cardinal.

"I expected this kind of question would come up. From what I've read in my short time reading parts of my library books and the Bible, it isn't entirely clear regarding God's wish toward gays and lesbians but you have to realize the writer could be interjecting his opinion in his writing. I don't think God physically took the hand of the writer and made it move on the paper. Anyway, in the Bible it states in Leviticus 18:22 says 'you shall not lie with a male as with a woman'. Romans 1:26 says 'females exchanged natural relations for unnatural relations and males likewise did shameful things with males'. 1 Corinthians 6:9 says 'Do you not know that the unjust will not inherit the kingdom of God? Do not be deceived; neither fornicators nor adulterers nor boy prostitutes nor practicing homosexuals nor thieves nor greedy nor drunkards nor slanderers nor robbers will inherit the kingdom of God'."

Bill continued, "but then I read in II Samual 1:26 'I grieve for you, Jonathon my brother! most dear have you been to me: More precious have I held love for you than love for women'. In Genesis 19 it seemingly isn't clear if Sodom and Gomora were destroyed because of homosexuality or social injustice. Translations from Hebrew were so inconsistent. For example, the Hebrew word for woman is ishsha and the Hebrew word for her man or her husband is ishah." The Cardinals noticed William was reading from several pages of notes.

"Where have you read all of that?" asked one of the Cardinals.

"The same place you should have read it," said William. "You supposedly are the learned ones. I'll list them for you in case you've missed them. It's *"The Popes"* by Rupert Matthews, *"The Vatican Diaries"* by John Thavis, *"Inside the Vatican"* by Thomas J. Reese, and the old standby *"Catholicism for Dummies"* by Rev. John Trigiligo., PhD, ThD and Rev. Kenneth Brighenti, PhD.

"You've caught a few of us unaware. I see you have a few notes, too." said Cardinal Whittier. "You've read quite a bit in your short time."

"Yes. In school we call it cramming. I knew I'd be speaking to learned men so I wanted to appear at least halfway educated. Also, like I said, I am currently leading a Bible study session for adults in my parish. I have learned several confusing items and some of our attendees have really brought up some interesting questions. I've been leading these sessions for three years now. Sometimes I surprise myself how many times Bible quotes pop into my head."

Some of the Cardinals smiled and some squirmed in their seats.

Cardinal Charlo asked, "Do you believe Jesus is the Son of God? Mary was a virgin? Do you believe the Apostles Creed?"

"Of course I do. In Cologne I had some very strict Catechism teachers."

The Cardinal continued, "Do you believe the Mass is exactly the same as Christ's sacrifice on Calvary?"

William said, "Yes. I believe the Mass simply doesn't represent Christ's death, it re-presents Christ's death."

"I'm impressed," said Cardinal Turner.

"This is getting us nowhere," said Cardinal Perez.

Cardinal Turner rose, "I think you're right, Josip. I think God, or we, have elected William to be our next Pope. Unless your detective friend finds out otherwise, he's our man."

Bill again looked around. "I don't think you gentlemen have been listening to me. I know very little about Church rules and regulations, I don't know anything about other denominations, I'm not a bishop or even a priest although I was a lay minister once and I am married with two children, and I was in line to be a deacon. I have a mortgage and car payments – I just can't do this pope thing. I am a policeman, a cop, a pig, or whatever you want to call me."

Cardinal Bendido asked, "William, surely you realize we are all sinners here."

"Yeah, but not like me."

"Different sins but sinners, William."

"William, about your home in Illinois, the diocese will handle those concerns," said Cardinal Whittier. "I think you are just what the Church needs. A fresh face. Someone from the real world. Someone not encumbered with our old pomp and circumstance. Someone who thinks outside the box."

"What does that mean?" asked Cardinal Peligrini.

"Oh Vincent, it means looking at things from a different perspective than the rest of us."

"William, would you not make a decision now," Cardinal Alverez said. "Talk it over with your wife. Your children are teenagers. Call them and see what they think. Many of our staff have teenage children. They go to school and play sports just like normal kids. Soccer is very big over here, like football is in the States."

"Rosalie is dead set against it. She is sure you will make us get a divorce."

"I don't think that would look good," said Cardinal Alverez. "We definitely won't do that. We have had enough scandalous Popes to have a divorced Pope too. We definitely want to promote a holy family life."

Bill added, "I read the Popes are supposed to know three or four languages. I remember a little German and Rosalie knows a little Italian."

"I've been thinking a lot about this whole circumstance," said Cardinal Pfeiffer. "We will be breaking a lot of new ground but just maybe it's what we need."

Cardinal Johnson said, "Maybe we're treading on old ground again."

Cardinal Raymundo rose. "I say let's have a show of hands here. Who will agree to ask William Joseph Meier III if he'll accept the position of Pope?"

"No! No! No! This is preposterous," said Cardinal Signorelli. Cardinal Stanlove shouted in agreement.

"I don't like it either," said Cardinal Perez, "but do you have a better idea?"

"Yes," said Cardinal Stanlove. "Call another Conclave."

"I see I'm causing a problem," said Bill weakly. "Why don't you just send Rosalie and me home?"

"God has spoken. Four times," said Cardinal Charlo. "It was unanimous. What more do you need?"

"But I didn't vote for him!" said Cardinal Signorelli slamming his fist on the table.

"But God did!"

Bill was getting quite embarrassed about the outbursts. "Gentlemen, let my wife and me go home, please."

Cardinal Madelo spoke, "William, as you can see, we Cardinals are quite human. Sometimes our discussions become heated. I won't mention any names but can you imagine us religious arguing over a parking space? But it happened."

"I know one of the parties involved," said Cardinal Signorelli sheepishly.

Cardinal Madelo continued, "William, you have stated several times you will not accept the vocation as Pope. Let's put it another way. This will settle the main question we Cardinals have. If Jesus Christ appeared in this room and asked you to be Pope, what would say to Him?"

Bill buried his head in his hands. Then he looked up to Cardinal Madelo. "Cardinal Madelo, your Eminence, do you really think God has performed this...I don't want to call it a miracle, this event?"

Cardinal Madelo said, "I don't know what to think. I agree Holy Mother the Church needs revitalizing. It needs new blood from outside the usual sources. It needs leadership from someone other than old Italians. Looking back to the early Church history Popes came from varied and eclectic bases. In the last five hundred years or so our choice of Popes was almost predictable. No one would ever expect a man from the United States to be elected to be Pope. In the early Church some Popes were married; some were not even bishops or priests. The last non-Cardinal elected pope was Pope Urban VI in 1378 and since 1276, until lately none have been non-European."

"Don't forget," someone said from the back of the chapel, "it brought about the Western Schism. The people wanted the election of Urban declared invalid. They said he was voted in due to fear of a mob. Cardinal Robert was voted in as Clement VII. We had two Popes. Then each pope excommunicated the other."

"Okay. I believe we're past all that," said Cardinal Pfeiffer. "Our rules have been made as we grew. Nearly every Pope has made changes in our procedures.In 1869 Pope Pius IX in the first Vatican Council declared the pope is infallible when it comes to God's teaching but interpretation unfortunately is by the seat of our pants. Our rules are as varied as Popes. Truly, if you accept the nomination as Pope, a lot of exemptions and exclusions will have to be put into place. It can be done but we'll have to have a majority of consent from Cardinals and bishops. I would have to know a lot more about you and your feelings regarding the status and teachings of the Church. Several changes implemented by previous Popes were met with approval by younger Christians and disapproval by our elder members. I hate to say this but there have times when we Cardinals didn't like our choices for Pope so we voted for a very old Cardinal knowing he wouldn't live very long. We hoped our choice would be better at a later date.

"In the early Church there were no Cardinals or bishops to choose a pope. The first popes were not bishops or even priests. Jesus didn't ordain anyone. A simple group of people choose a pope. And then there were even arguments and fights over the decision. Each group would name their own favorite as pope. At one time even three men were named as pope and even a woman was named although she hid her gender.

"We'd have to weigh the possibilities whether the Church would grow or wane. Do we immediately ordain you as a priest and then bishop or do we design a new and novel definition of the Vicar of Christ; a new definition of the Holy See? William, the appearance of your name on our ballots is to me most exciting and yet frightful. Does God see in you something both invigorating and yet comfortable? Does He see someone who can attract new followers and retain old members? Don't make a decision yet, William. As we said, talk it over with Rosalie and your sons. And to my brethren in this Chapel, we have to decide how we would administer to our congregations with a layman as Pope. I think I have talked enough."

Cardinal Perez said, "I agree. You have given quite a homily Oswald, but I will state again. I do not think William should accept. I am sure my detective friend will find out how this farce, this lunacy, has occurred. By the time you head back to the States we'll have an answer. I am sure, William, you have not precipitated this incident but someone has and we'll get to the bottom of it."

The elder Cardinal Marshall said, "Let's have a show of hands. Who thinks William should accept the position of Pope?"

"No!" shouted Cardinal Perez.

"Let's put it this way," said Cardinal Marshall. "First, those in favor of William accepting raise your hand."

Sixty Cardinals raised their hand.

"Now, those against, raise your hand."

Seventeen Cardinals raised their hand.

"Those who have not yet made a decision, raise your hand."

Thirty-four Cardinals raised their hand. Cardinal Balino was absent. Several Cardinals refused to vote.

"This is pure madness," said Cardinal Stanlove.

Cardinal Marshall said, "Should I have the secretary contact the Cardinals not present to ascertain their position?"

"There's no need for this," said Cardinal Whittier. "We have a majority."

"Cardinal Balino is not here and several ill Cardinals have retired for the day but, yes, go ahead," said Cardinal Perez. "William, I will contact Father Thiel and have him bring your wife over here. I'll have Father take you to the cafeteria for lunch. I'd like you and your wife to return to your apartment and talk things over. The rest of us will go to lunch and return here. We have many items to discuss. Let's say a closing prayer and depart."

CHAPTER EIGHT

Cardinal Perez looked at the gathered group of Cardinals. He did not know where to begin. "My brethren, I am not sure how we should address our dilemma. I know most of you have to get home soon. I don't think we accomplished much this morning. Do we dare assume this is a directive from God? If it is, we shouldn't be wasting all this afternoon discussing if William should be installed as Pope. I don't like it one bit as I have said several times. We have several avenues to take to make his Papacy operational. Looking back at our history, there have been occasions where the Pope was a layman. Before there was a Conclave, the Pope was chosen by acclamation. William would have the College of Bishops, the Synod of Bishops, the Roman Curia and us, the College of Cardinals to guide any decision or edict he would issue. We would have to admit there would be some protection of each organization's turf as the Americans say. We would have to appoint someone to be the Bishop of Rome. We'd have to have several Canon Lawyers accompany William at all times. If this is truly the finger of the Holy Spirit pointing to William von Meier III, we should, we must, obey Him. If it is trick or hoax, I should know soon. I truly have no fear. My detective will find out how this happened and this whole dilemma will be a moot point. Any thoughts about this?"

Cardinal Paulo spoke, "Josip, you know how I feel. It is truly a hoax, possibly a work of the Devil. There is no way this man should be appointed Pope. I will resist until my dying day."

"Fredrico," Cardinal Perez said, "I know how you feel. I am sure you were aware I was vying for the vote to be Pope but I am ready to give in for the moment – that is until my detective finds trickery. And I am sure he will."

"You haven't even met with your detective yet."

"He's a busy man," said Cardinal Perez, "but I hope to meet with him next week."

The door to the chapel opened and Cardinal Salvatore Balino walked in. "Good afternoon my brethren. Sorry I couldn't be here sooner. I was visiting my brother who is quite ill and just got the message from our secretary of your, or should I say, our problem. How are we doing?"

"Salvatore, we have a problem and our modern Church has too much bureaucracy built into it to settle the predicament."

"I agree," said the Cardinal. "The early Church would just say, 'William, you're elected Pope' and that would be it. Maybe that's your answer. There'd be enough of us to implement checks and balances on the man."

"I see the secretary has brought you up to date, Salvatore."

Cardinal Balino added, "What if Jesus appeared in this room and said, 'Let William Joseph von Meier III be Pope.' Would any of you argue?"

"We've asked that question before," said Cardinal Mancino."

"What was your answer?"

"We didn't answer it."

Cardinal Balino said, "Let's get his outlook on our pertinent problems affecting us at this moment. If they don't seem too radical, let's name the man Pope."

Cardinal Cesario said, "He also said he wouldn't accept the position."

"If God truly chose him, we must convince him to accept."

"I think the answer is simple," said Cardinal Signorelli. "Let's just let him refuse."

Cardinal Whittier spoke up. "No. I feel God has chosen William. We will have to convince him to accept. I think he would be a great Pope – of course after we sound him out thoroughly regarding his opinions about the Church. I think he has the potential to be a great leader."

"You would say that, Peter," said Cardinal Stanlove. "Your diocese is in Illinois. Isn't that where Peoria is?"

"That has no bearing on my opinion, but I think we all agree we have never had a non-European Pope."

"Rubbish!" said Cardinal Perez. "Let us make a list of problems we have with our Church. We will present them to William tomorrow."

"A waste of time," said Cardinal Signorelli. "This man is a policeman. A cop. Why even consider him by discussing any Church problems with him. I think you wasted money even bringing him and his wife to Rome. We gave him a free tour of the Vatican. I agree we have had some terrible Popes but let us not add another one.

Meanwhile Father Thiel returned William to his apartment. Rosalie was waiting for him. "Did you tell them?"

"Not actually. We can talk after lunch."

Before they left for lunch, Bill gathered his library books regarding the Vatican. "Look at these, Father.Have you read any of them? I presented them to the Cardinals."

"No, I haven't," said Father. "I should add I am still studying."

"Some are quite shocking."

"I can imagine," said the priest. "In our studies we've been introduced to many exposé and Vatican Secrets books, but not these particular ones."

"Reading them just makes me want to be Pope and correct our few faults. What if that is what God wants me to do?"

"Bill," said Rosalie. "You haven't answered me. You're going to accept, aren't you?"

"I told them I wouldn't accept. They just did not seem to listen to me," said Bill.

"I called the boys," said Rosalie. "I didn't realize it but I woke them up."

"Good. What are their thoughts on the situation?"

Rosalie sat down in the cafeteria. "Bill, they're all for it. They talked to Father Johnston and he's more excited than the boys. They went over to the rectory and Father explained to them how confusing and unorthodox early Popes were chosen. How will you get out of this?"

"I don't know," said Bill. "That's all the boys had to say?"

"Oh no. They wanted to know if the pizza was the same as in the states. They asked about soccer. Bill, they said to tell Dad to do it."

"Rosalie, they asked me this question. What would I do if Jesus appeared and personally asked me to be Pope?"

"What did you say?"

"I didn't answer. I avoided it. I changed the subject."

Rosalie said, "Bill, you have to tell them you are going to refuse."

As they left the cafeteria Father Thiel quickly scanned Bill's books. "You've got to make your own decision Bill."

Bill took his library books and said, "Look at the articles explaining the Vatican politics. It's almost ludicrous. Rosalie, what if God wants me to be the Pope? What if God thinks I can lead the Church? What if the Holy Spirit thinks I can make the Church more transparent and less inflexible? Look at the scandals the Vatican has had recently?

"Bill, yes or no?" Bill didn't answer.

Father Thiel left the couple at their apartment still in discussion.

As they entered their living room, Bill said, "Okay Rosalie, what should I say to Jesus if He asked me to be Pope?"

"Bill no! You can't do this. I'd never see you again. It would tear our marriage apart."

"Do you think the Cardinals would want a divorced Pope? Do you think Jesus would want a divorced Pope leading His sheep? There is too much divorce in the world now. Christ wouldn't want the leader of over one billion Catholics to be divorced. And Rosalie my dear, I wouldn't want that or let that happen. You will be at my side – always."

"Sure. What will the world think seeing a woman hugging the Pope wearing all those fancy vestments and stuff?"

"Rosalie, they are preparing a bunch of questions to ask me tomorrow. They still might not offer me the position. You know? They almost came to blows in the Chapel. The Cardinals are human, just like us. They fought over a parking space. Can you believe it?"

"I don't know what to say."

"Do you know what else?" Bill continued, "I always thought the Catholic Church rules and regulations were cut and dried – the same since Jesus's time. They aren't and they weren't. These Cardinals don't even agree on things we always thought were set. I've read that some of the Cardinals don't believe Mary gave birth to Jesus in a virgin birth. Some do not believe the soul is created at the moment of conception. They interpret the Bible differently. I don't think Jesus would recognize His Church today."

Rosalie asked Bill again. "Bill, for the third time, are you going to accept or not?"

"There are several Cardinals dead set against me being named Pope."

"Bill, what about our mortgage payment and car payment and credit card debt? What about your job and your pension and retirement? I can just hear the chief telling the other policemen that Bill left the force to be Pope. Bill, we have all of our clothes and pictures and furniture and my art supplies at home. Can we bring our new stove and refrigerator? How do we bring that overseas? What about our car?" Suddenly Rosalie started laughing.

"What so funny?" asked Bill.

"This is so ridiculous it's comical. Three weeks ago our Social Justice Group was praying that the new Pope would update and modernize the Church. Now, you're the one that might be bringing our Church to contemporary times." Rosalie laughed even harder. Wiping tears from her eyes she said, "Bill, let's do it. I might even remember some Italian. My parents have died but I may have some relatives here. At least we don't have any in the States."

"Yes, we've both lost our parents."

Bill walked over to Rosalie and hugged her. "Well, I expected some kind of response but not this." Bill began laughing too.

"What would the process be for you to become pope?" asked Rosalie.

"They told me all would be taken care of, that is, if they officially offer me the job, or position or whatever they call it." Bill was laughing too.

"Bill, do really think God is asking you to be Pope? If He is, it is scary to think God is touching you on the shoulder. Is the Church in such bad shape that He wants you to straighten it out? What do you know that is so important to the Church? Bill! What if you're a saint? I'm standing next to a saint. I should bow down and pray to you."

"Oh come on, Rosalie. Don't be ridiculous." Bill started laughing again.

Rosalie began laughing even harder. "I can't help it. St. William of Peoria. "

"I don't know anything out of the ordinary. There are many things about the Church I don't like. Many things seem stupid or lack common sense."

Still giggling Rosalie said, "Like what"

"The way the Church treats women, birth control, confession in a closet, celibacy for priests to name a few. A biggy is how so much money is spent on pomp and circumstance when it could help the poor."

Rosalie said to Bill, "I didn't know you thought that seriously about the Church. I thought you just thought about police work. Didn't you always say you wanted to be a detective?"

"I know but some of the things the late Pope said bothered me. I was hoping we'd get a more progressive Pope. I never thought it'd be me."

"I don't know what to say, Bill."

"Another biggy to me is how the Church treats sex. I just don't like the way they treat intercourse as a terrible, vile and despicable deed. Did you know in the early Church a married Pope was forbidden to have intercourse with his wife? There's no proof the popes adhered to the rule. Even married couples had to go to confession before receiving Holy Communion.

"For goodness sake, God made the act. That is how He planned to continue the human race. Over and over again they keep saying how Mary was a virgin before and after Christ was born. God could surely accomplish a virgin birth if He so desired but why does the Church say repeatedly she remained a virgin afterward. Why does that make her less of a holy woman if she was no longer a virgin? And then they say repeatedly again that Jesus didn't have any brothers or sisters. I read in the Bible Matthew 13:55 they even named his brothers and admitted he had sisters. The church repeatedly says what the writers meant was that those were Jesus's disciples. That doesn't make sense because Jesus had just begun His ministry. I don't think He had chosen His disciples yet."

"Is that what you're getting out of all those library books?"

Bill said, "Yeah. Do you know years ago we were forbidden to read some of these books? The holy leaders were afraid we'd misunderstand them. I think what they were really afraid of is that we would understand them."

Rosalie looked Bill in the eye, "William, admit it. You actually want the job, don't you?"

"It's sure a fascinating possibility. Anyway, we have to make up our minds soon. Do we fly back to the States as simple lay people or Pope and Popess?"

"Popess. Will I have to wear fancy garb, too?"

In their room, Bill sat on the bed, holding one of his Vatican library books. "I get the feeling if I accept they are going to have to make up a lot of new procedures and rituals."

"Bill. Just think of this. This is serious stuff. If God really called you to be Pope, He must have some really important things for you to do. We can't take this lightly."

"But what if it is a hoax?"

"Then we will just have to play it out and trust in God."

Bill stood up and looked out to a small garden. "Your faith is so much stronger than mine."

"If you accept I am going to stand right beside you. The world is going to know you are a married man- or married Pope."

"We have three days until our Sunday flight home. Let's hope we get a sign showing us what to do."

CHAPTER NINE

Thursday morning came much too soon for Bill and Rosalie. They assumed it was Father Thiel knocking on their door.

"Ready William? Sister will take you, Mrs. Meier, to see all of our museums. I'm sure you'll enjoy them."

"Will I get to meet the Cardinals?" asked Rosalie.

Father Thiel noticed Rosalie seemed in a better frame of mind today. "I'm sure you will, Mrs. Meier. What did you think of our gardens? Did you know we have 108.7 acres and the Vatican grounds are nearly half garden?"

"No, I didn't. I guess I'll see you at lunch, Bill."

Once again Father Thiel and Sister Rose Williams carried their passengers off in different directions.

"I can't get over the fact that I'll soon be calling you 'Your Holiness'."

"I don't know, Father," said Bill. "If this is the real thing, if God is truly calling me, then I am just about ready to panic. How did you get your calling?"

"Not as dramatic as yours. I was driving to town to pick up my girlfriend, Katheryn, and I was thinking about my parish priest, Father Wilhelm, telling me I should think about the priesthood. I jokingly said out loud to God, 'Give me a sign' and He did. On the road ahead of me I saw an auto on the side of the road with its hood up. I stopped to help and it was my parish priest, Father Wilhelm. He said John, I knew God would send me a good person to help and sure enough he did. That was all I needed. I called Katheryn and told her. I told her I was going to answer God's call to be a priest. End of story."

"Did you think of refusing?"

"Definitely. But then I thought what if that was Jesus with a broken down auto. Could I refuse Him? No way."

Bill thought to himself, could I refuse Him – in a broken down auto? No way. Once again they arrived at the Chapel.

"Thanks, Father," said Bill. "I think I just got a sign."

Cardinal Perez was standing at the door waiting for him. "Come in, William. I hope you and Mrs. Meier had a comfortable evening."

"Thank you, your Eminence, "said Bill. "We did. We strolled through some of the garden areas."

"Yes, that is one of the things that surprises most tourists."

Bill was again overwhelmed by so many Cardinals in the small chapel. William said, "Besides painting, Rosalie's other hobby is gardening."

Bill sat again toward the front of the chapel. Cardinal Perez was about to speak when a Cardinal in the back of the chapel rose and spoke. "Josip, may I say something before we begin?"

"Yes, Michael."

"If I may respectfully say, I think this is a waste of time. I feel God – or the Holy Spirit – has spoken four times to us. I feel also this is...let's say, a miracle. I trust this is a man God feels can guide us. When we choose..."

Cardinal Signorelli interrupted Cardinal Reardon, "I feel you are a fool, Michael. I say let's just have a simple show of hands, the way it was done in early Church history. There is no way a trickster or magician can manipulate our hands. We simply count hands and I assure you no one is going to make me raise my hand to elect this cop to be Pope."

Cardinal Whittier spoke up. "My brethren. I am reminded of the old joke about the drowning man. He prayed to God to save him. Along came a boat and the operator offered to bring him aboard. He refused saying, 'God will save me.' Another bigger boat came along and he again refused saying, 'God will save me.' Finally the man drowned. When coming before God's throne he asked God, 'Why didn't you save me?' God said, 'I sent you two boats but you refused their help.' Do we want to take a chance and drown? I think this is a boat we should take. Let's waste no more time. Announce to the world we have chosen our new Pope. If we are mistaken, Josip, your detective will find out and we'll then declare the election invalid. It will be an honest mistake and no one will blame us."

"Peter, you're still trying to get your man from Illinois elected," said Cardinal Signorelli.

Cardinal Perez said, "Be still, Giovani. I guess there is some merit in what Peter is saying. I'm not comfortable with this circumstance but maybe we will have to trust God that this is truly a message from Him. Quite honestly I will do all in my power to have this election declared invalid. But for now, let's have a show of hands. We need a two-thirds majority. In the thirteenth century in the town of Viterbo it took two years and nine months to elect a successor to Clement IV. The populous put quite a bit of pressure on the Cardinals. They cut their food rations, then gave them only bread and water. Then they took away their servants, took away the firewood for heating and cooking and even tore the roof off their building when it was raining. Let's not take that long. Who thinks we should announce to the world that William Joseph von Meier III is out next Pope – if William agrees?"

The Cardinals began shifting in their seats and looking around at each other. Cardinal Perez slowly raised his hand. Thirty hands quickly followed Cardinal Perez's action. A few more raised their hands, and then a few more. Soon at least half the Cardinals had raised their hands. Then a few more raised their hands.

After counting the hands, finally Cardinal Perez spoke, "Well William, we have over two thirds. It is up to you. Do you want to be the leader of over a billion Catholics?"

Bill's head was reeling. He suddenly felt as if he were in a dream. Can this really be happening? Me? A Pope? A few days ago I was remodeling my bathroom. Now, I'm in Rome. In the Vatican. How could this happen? He said, "Wait. I have to talk to Rosalie. I have to know... I don't know what to do. Don't I have to be a priest and bishop? I have to know the rules and regulations. What's this Canon Law you talk about?

"This is serious," he continued. "Do I have to wear the fancy vestments? I only know English and a little German. What if I make a mistake? What if I commit a sin? Sometimes I use the name of God in vain. I have a habit of swearing. This is a heavy responsibility. Do I get any training? The Church has problems right now and I'll probably add to them. I will have to give answers and solutions."

"I see you already have a feel for what the Church needs," said Cardinal McMillan. "So, what's your answer? Yes or no?"

"I have a lot of work to do," said Bill.

"Not half as much as we have to do," said Cardinal Whittier. "We have to sell our selection to our Catholic community. I know Illinois will be thrilled but the rest of the world – especially Italy – will not be happy. I don't know if we'll lose or gain followers but we will have to trust God."

"Oh my God," was all Bill could say.

Cardinal Whittier spoke again, "William, do you have any feeling that God may have an idea that you may be a source of solutions to the problems of our Church? Father Johnston checked on your grades at the community college you attended in Illinois. He said you were at the top of your class so I feel you are an intelligent man."

"Those were easy classes, Cardinal."

"What's your feeling about abortion?"

"As I said earlier, it's murder when performed because it is an inconvenient pregnancy. As far as rape or incest or because of a malformed fetus, I don't know. I know we cannot play God and bring death to a fetus, the same as euthanasia. I would have to ask scholars much more learned than I to have an answer. I can refute one of the women's rights arguments though. They argue it's their body and they can do what they want with it. Here's a news flash for them. It's not their body. It has an entirely different set of genes. I repeat, it's not part of their body. It's a completely different human being. They are killing a human."

"I like that thought, " said Cardinal Whittier. "What about priest celibacy?"

"It's foolish. St. Peter was married as were many early priests, bishops and even Popes. I heard many arguments either way but common sense tells us it might eliminate many pedophiles in the Church - and not just pedophiles but the occasional liaisons between priests and female parishioners. Look how many mistresses have been secretly kept in the past – even in the present – in our Church."

"What are you saying?" yelled Cardinal Randondi.

William looked directly at the Cardinal. For the first time Bill seemed a little perturbed. "You know what I mean, Cardinal. There are more leaks in your little kingdom than a sieve."

Cardinal Paulo said, "William, don't forget to whom you are speaking."

William stood a little straighter. "Cardinal, I've been attempting a crash course of Vatican history, Vatican secrets and Vatican politics. Things go on in big corporations such a GM or Ford but they are somewhat transparent. Things go on in the Vatican but you seem to cover it up with many forms of concealment. I can even see some hypocrisy." Now Bill was even letting some anger be displayed. "You have gays interspersed in your clergy at this moment. You have affairs going on. May I say even in your band of Cardinals."

Cardinal Perez screamed, "HOW DARE YOU!"

Cardinal Whittier said, "Do you want to argue the point, Josip?"

"I'm leaving," said Cardinal Perez.

"You'll miss all the fun," said Cardinal Johnson. "We might even talk about you."

Still fuming the Cardinal slowly sat back down.

"Gentlemen, or should I say Brethren," said William. "I don't want to insinuate that our clergy is full of sinners. I didn't mean to sound that way. I am sure out of the many thousands of clergy men and women throughout the world only a very few are offenders of God's law. The press loves to single us out when one of us fail."

Cardinal Randondi voiced at a slightly higher pitch, "I think we've heard enough. This man can never be Pope. I don't care if Jesus Christ himself came down and pointed to Mr. von Meier."

Cardinal Marshall, an elder, slowly walked up to the front of the Chapel. "My Brethren, I see a precedent here. I move we ordain William von Meier III to the priesthood and then to be bishop. And since Cardinal Balino speaks Italian, I also move to appoint Salvatore to be acting Bishop of Rome for the time being. There is no written rule saying we cannot do this. Holy Mother the Church has had so many rule changes over the centuries I don't see how or why we should remain so rigid and stoic regarding naming William Pope. Every Pope we have had down through the centuries has made little adjustments to suit their whims. In 1854 Pope Pius IX suddenly decided Popes were infallible. He stated the virginity of Mary was an article of faith, which is admirable, but it was his choice. God can truly do whatever He wants. There's even disagreement on Mary's virginity. "

A slight uproar was heard in the Sistine Chapel. There were voices of approval and disapproval. This time William did not ask to be dismissed. He thought it most amusing seeing the men of God acting so human and displaying antics he has witnessed in meetings at the Police Department back in Illinois.

Cardinal Perez pounded his fist on his desk. "Gentlemen of God! What are you doing? This is not a United Nations meeting. I want a show of hands. Who votes to elect William Joseph von Meier III to be Pope?

Ninety Cardinals raised their hands.

"Who votes to not elect William Joseph von Meier III to be Pope?"

Twenty-six Cardinals raised their hands.

"Mr. William Joseph Meier III, do you accept the selection of the College of Cardinals?"

Bill said weakly, "I would like to ask Rosalie."

"What?" said Cardinal Perez.

"I would humbly request I be Pope without being ordained as bishop or priest."

Someone asked, "Can this be done?"

"No!" said Cardinal Perez. "It's a rule the man elected must be a bishop or priest."

"It's an unwritten rule, Josip," said a Cardinal. "It can be done. Even some early Cardinals were not bishops or priests."

"I know Rosalie well enough. She won't object. My answer is yes."

"Father John," said Cardinal Perez. "take William to his apartment now."

In a somewhat belated action, Cardinal Perez said, "Send up white smoke. I feel Mr. Candelo will soon solve our problem. I am sure there is some trickery going on and he will bring it to light. Then the election of Mr. William Joseph von Meier III will be a moot point and we can send him and his wife tramping back to the States. Until then, as said in the States, we will keep him on a short leash."

After Cardinal Signorelli and Cardinal Perez were alone, Cardinal Signorelli said, "I don't think this is a good idea. Is this detective friend of yours any good? Is he expensive and where are you getting the money?"

"He's a good Catholic," said Cardinal Perez with his fingers crossed. "I doubt he'll charge us anything. He wants this puzzle solved as much as we do. I'll give him enough to cover his expenses.' Then laughing heartily he said, "I'll give him a plenary indulgence for any future sins."

"I don't see anything funny about this, Josip."

Cardinal Perez said, "Lighten up, Giovani. I guarantee this is no goddamn miracle. Mr. Candelo will solve our dilemma."

"And another thing, Josip," said Cardinal Signorelli. "I don't like your language lately."

"Just relax. I'm taking care of everything. Go take care of your sheep."

CHAPTER TEN

William returned to his apartment. He faced Rosalie. "Bill," said Rosalie. "I heard a bunch of bells around here. I think I know what it means. You've accepted the appointment or whatever. You're going to be the next Pope, aren't you?"

"Yes."

Rosalie looked William in the eye. "Do you know what that means?"

"No, I don't really know, yet. I am really scared, Rosalie. If God actually picked me to be Pope He must know something about me I don't even know. If my name was miraculously written on those ballots then God must have been present right there, in the Sistine Chapel. He must feel I have a responsibility or ability to do something great. But I have no idea what it could be. Over a billion Catholics are waiting for the next Pope to do something great. As soon as I pick a name, I am the next Pope. Will God put great ideas in my brain? Or if I fail, will I have an especially low place in Hell?"

Rosalie said slowly, "Bill, I just don't know what to say. Will our marriage be annulled?"

"No, no. There have been several married Popes, just none lately. It's just one of the many unwritten rules asserted lately. Our marriage will remain intact. That's the least of my concerns. What I am thinking of is my many opinions about the Church. Think of the many times I've ranted and raved about the ridiculous edicts published by the Vatican. Remember how I've spouted off about the lack of common sense coming out of Rome regarding birth control? Is God saying? 'Hey Bill, those are some good ideas there! Let's announce them'."

Rosalie said, "I go from laughing to crying. This is a dream or maybe a nightmare."

"What scares me the most, Rosalie, is that some of my rantings about the Church are possibly blasphemous. What would happen if I go out there and espouse something entirely immoral?"

"I know you wouldn't do that, Bill," said Rosalie. "Oh Bill. Will I have to stop calling you Bill?" Rosalie giggled and then suddenly stopped. "Will I have to call you 'Your Holiness?"

"I don't think so, at least not in private. But listen, I'll have to name bishops and archbishops and Cardinals. I'll have to name saints. Oh my God, and I mean it. I can't do this. I can't. There's so much fighting and warring in the world. There's poverty and sickness. I'll be expected to say great things all around the world."

There was a knock on the door. Rosalie answered it. It was Father Thiel. "Let's go to lunch, your Holiness. You too, Mrs. von Meier."

"Oh! Am I dressed okay?"

"You're fine," said Father. "There is a problem about how to dress the Pope." He looked at William and smiled.

"I guess no more jeans?"

"Yes, I believe so," said Father, "but you'll have to wear something appropriate when you address the throngs on the balcony tomorrow."

"What?"

"Your first speech. All Popes do it. I am extremely curious about the reaction you'll get. I've inquired around the Vatican grounds and most employees are overjoyed. A few of the older Italians are not, though. Quite a large crowd of people, as well as the press, have been waiting, almost patiently I might add, for your greeting to your people. You'll greet them tomorrow from your balcony."

"I think I'll dress just like the Cardinals did today. Just in black, minus the red sash. I hope I don't throw up."

Father Thiel laughed, "By the way. Cardinal Perez and several other Cardinals want to meet with you and Mrs. von Meier this afternoon after lunch. I'm to bring you both over to their office."

"Oh, oh. Now it begins," said William.

Bill and Rosalie fretfully ate their lunch.

After lunch, Bill and Rosalie cautiously entered the office of Cardinal Perez. Like many other offices, shelves of books lined the room. Similarly, his desk was covered with piles of papers and folders. The furnishings were rather plush. As to be expected, many pictures of Popes and Saints lined the walls. The windows were covered with heavy dark drapes and the carpet was quite plush. Several other Cardinals were already seated in the office but William did not remember their names from the morning's meeting. The Cardinals were a blur of old men. In the background some operatic soprano was singing her heart out. William guessed the recording was in Italian

Cardinal Perez greeted the highly intimidated couple. "Come in and have a seat. Hello Mrs. von Meier. How are you holding up?"

"Not too well, I'm afraid," said Rosalie. "I go from thinking my husband is the receiver of some miracle from God to thinking he's the butt of some cruel joke to... I don't know what."

"I can understand. Let me introduce you to Cardinal Andrew Di Magio and Cardinal Peter Whittier. Cardinal Whittier is from Illinois."

"I know," said Rosalie.

"And this is Sister Rose Williams. She'll be your aid, secretary, chauffeur and whatever else you might need."

Rosalie said, "I know. She's been driving me around the last few days."

"Fine. Let's get down to business. I'll get right to the point. Do you think your husband should accept the election results? Should he become our next Pope?"

"Sir... Oh, your Eminence. I am leaving that decision completely up to William. I personally am completely overwhelmed by this whole experience. Suddenly we have been catapulted from oblivion to world-wide notoriety. I am suddenly afraid to go outside the Vatican walls. I am actually afraid to go out of my room. Everyone is looking at me like they expect me to make a mistake. But again, whatever William decides, I'll abide with. I just hope the children and I can be by his side always."

Cardinal Perez walked over to Rosalie. "I can assure you, Mrs. von Meier, we will always want you by his side. I am sure God likes families and He, and I, would want you and your family to always show an example of a Christian family life. It would be somewhat like Jesus, Mary and Joseph. We'd have Rosalie, William, David and Charles."

Cardinal Wittier rolled his eyes to heaven. "Josip, let me say a few things."

"Sure, Peter."

"William – and if you still intend to accept the election, your Holiness – let me answer a few of your questions. As far as your home, Bishop Cartwright tells me it's across the street from the church. The parish needs another building for some religion classes, training facilities and some other uses. With your permission, we would take over its use. We'd pay utilities, insurance, taxes and mortgage – if there is one."

"Yes, there is," said William.

"We'd be setting a precedent. We would keep it in some kind of trust for you if things don't work out here. We've also talked to your police union representative. If you die as Pope, your retirement would go to your wife and children."

William interrupted, "You've talked to my union? Have you talked to my chief, too?"

"We've talked to as many friends, relatives, fellow workers and business associates as possible. Without fail, everyone said you are the most honest, down to earth, Christian gentleman they know. One thing that really interested me was what your chief said. He said a joke was going around the station. The man telling the joke said even Bill wouldn't be offended. That speaks well of your Christian upbringing. Oh, and I assured them you'd be the one to let them know of your final decision whether or not to lead the Roman Catholic Church."

"Do I get a salary?"

"No. But you won't need one. Everything is paid for, for you and your family - within reason, of course. And, if you fly to some country, your wife and children may accompany you if they choose."

William asked, "Cardinal, do you really think I am the recipient of some miracle from God? What an awesome responsibility God has handed me if this is true."

"Unless Josip's detective friend returns with evidence to the contrary, we will have to believe it's a miracle, although 'miracle' is not the word we want to use. We still have some reservations but stranger miracles have occurred. How about the miracle Jesus worked when Peter couldn't pay the temple tax?"

"Really?" asked William. "I don't remember that one."

"It's in Matthew 17:27. Jesus said, 'But that we may not offend them (the tax collectors), go to the sea, drop in a hook, and take the first fish that comes up. Open its mouth and you will find a coin worth twice the temple tax'."

William said, "That's surely is a weird miracle."

"So weird many of the early Popes obsessed in regard to finances and constantly prayed for a similar miracle. It never happened."

"So, if I accept, can I set down some conditions, some parameters?"

Cardinal Whittier spoke up, "Surely, if they are within reason. What might they be?"

"Since I won't be a bishop or priest I do not want to wear those flowing garments and custom fitted vestments."

"I suppose some arrangements can and will be made. Popes usually wear white."

"Also, since I won't be ordained, I will need a priest or bishop or maybe a Cardinal always at my side to dispense blessings. Hopefully we can call them Vatican Blessings instead of Papal Blessings."

Cardinal Perez smiled. "Don't you worry. I will always be at your side. I, and a Canon Lawyer, will be there. A lot depends on how our congregation accepts you. I believe many emotions may be revealed. Perhaps a lot of consternation, anger, dread, possibly fear and maybe even joy. Who knows what your reception will be after you are introduced."

William began to feel some of the anger and anxiety developing right here in the College of Cardinals. "I suppose I will have to give some speech from the balcony. Can I have Father Thiel as my aid or assistant and chauffeur?"

"Oh, I will write your speech for you," said Cardinal Perez. "and I'll assign someone else as your personal aid."

William did not like the tone of Cardinal Perez's voice but he remained silent for a moment. "I'll need someone to translate to Italian. My wife will be there, too. She is quickly becoming fluent in the language again and will soon be able to help me. John is helping me to again become proficient in German."

Rosalie sat in silence.

"As I said, I will assign another priest to be your assistant, and chauffeur." Cardinal Perez displayed some annoyance at the mention of Father Thiel, especially calling the priest by his first name.

"Cardinal Perez," asked William. "When am I officially the Pope?"

"The moment you accepted this morning. Are you having second thoughts?"

William glanced at Rosalie and said, "No, I accept." She displayed no emotion.

Under his breath, Cardinal Perez said, "I was afraid of that."

William said, "Cardinal Perez, Josip, the way I see it, I will make my speech to the people so my acceptance will be public knowledge. Then I will need to go back to the states and close my affairs. My wife and I, and my children, will have to make arrangements to have our valuables and personal items shipped here. Oh, and my boys will need passports. That shouldn't take more than one or two weeks, don't you agree?" Cardinal Perez seemed to be quite uncomfortable at William's using his first name. He also seemed uneasy at William's taking charge of the situation.

"Yes, I suppose so."

"Then, let's get on with it." The phrase 'loose cannon' began rambling around in Cardinal Perez's brain. Cardinal Whittier smiled.

"You and Mrs. Meier can return to you room. Your apartment is still being prepared and will be ready tomorrow. You will give your speech from the balcony as usual. Arrangements are being made for your flight back to the United States."

As Bill and Rosalie climbed into their shuttle vehicle, they were surprised at Cardinal Whittier climbing in with them. "We'll talk a bit, if that's okay with you, your Holiness?"

"That'd be great. I need a confidant and I hoped it would be you. I understand you speak Italian. You could help Rosalie get proficient in the language. Father Thiel has been terrific. Can I retain him?"

"You can," said Cardinal Wittier. "It's entirely your decision. You're going to find some strong politics in action here. That's some of what I wanted to talk to you about. I have a hunch the

Church needs you. I am very excited about the future of the Roman Catholic Church with you as our leader."

"Cardinal," said William. "It just plain seems arrogant or pretentious to act or speak as though I am the Pope. I remember a few times you visited our parish back home; I was hesitant to look you in the eye. You are God's official messenger and who was I to look at you. I was a simple sinner standing before God's representative. Rosalie and I loved how down to earth you were. "

Cardinal Whittier said, "Thank you. William, you may, and should, call me Peter. You're going to have to get used to being in charge. Unless Josip's detective finds otherwise, you are Christ's representative - and I doubt detective so-and-so will find anything. As we say back home, you are 'the man'. I feel confident you can be Pope and not appear lordly or pompous."

"I will try," said William. "Can you stay here in Rome to help me or do you have to go back to Illinois?"

Cardinal Whittier smiled. "Your Holiness, it is your decision. You tell me and I will obey. Just like the Roman soldier with the sick child told Christ. I too have subjects under me. I tell them to go and they go. I tell them to stay and they stay. Do you want to assign me here in Rome?"

"Do you mind? Would you like to stay?"

Cardinal Whittier said, "We take a vow of obedience, poverty and chastity. This might seem odd for a young man your age but obedience is the hardest. Yes, I'd like to be assigned here but you could also assign me to the South Pole and I'd like it - although not as much as here in Rome. Remember though, you will then have to assign someone to be a Cardinal back home."

"Oh my God. Oops," said William. "That's another thing, Cardinal - I mean Peter - I use bad language sometimes."

"We are still human beings. That's why we go to confession at least once a week."

The shuttle vehicle reached William and Rosalie's quarters. "John, if you don't mind, I am going to assign you as my aid and chauffeur. Is that okay?"

Father Thiel laughed. "Did you hear what the Cardinal said? You could assign me to the South Pole too and I'd accept."

William said, "I definitely will need a secretary, or secretaries."

"Even Peter had secretaries," said Cardinal Whittier. "In Romans 16:22 Peter says, 'Tertius, the writer of this letter, greet you in the Lord'. And in 1 Peter 5:12, he says 'I write you this briefly through Silvanus whom I consider my faithful brother,...' You'll need a lot of help to be a good leader."

"I guess I am a weak leader."

Rosalie laughed too. "I've heard you give orders to some of your officers under you. You're not a weak leader."

"Yes, your Holiness. You'll have to become somewhat assertive," said Cardinal Whittier.

William opened the door to their room. A maid was in the room straightening up and dusting.

"Oh," said the maid. "Your Holiness. I was just leaving."

"That's fine," said William. "Take your time."

"I am so honored to meet you and be cleaning your room," she said in broken English. "I hope I can do so again."

"What is your name?" asked Rosalie.

"Lucretia," she said.

"We'll see what arrangements can be made," said William. "I'd like to have you be the one to care for our papal apartment when we move over there."

"Oh thank you, your Holiness." The maid left the room.

CHAPTER ELEVEN

William, Rosalie and Cardinal Whittier found some comfortable chairs in their apartment and made themselves at home. The Cardinal picked up some of the library books Bill had brought with him from home.

"I see you brought some Vatican reading material with you," said the Cardinal. "Have you been reading them?"

"Yes I have," said William. "I should say I am shocked by some of the things I have read but then again, maybe I am naïve. After listening to some of the discussions and arguments by the Cardinals I am not surprised."

Cardinal Whittier sat upright. "May I call you William?

"My gosh, your Eminence, I mean Peter, yes."

"William, the Vatican is full of humans. By that I mean a lot of the common problems and frailties we have we try to veil from the world but those faults, sins and iniquities are still present. You must get over thinking things in Vatican are all holy and sacred. Only living in one generation we sometimes think the Church has always been this way. People think the Church is an inflexible, rigid business. As you read these books - and I recognize some of them - you may be shocked at some of the failings of our early clergy. I've recognized in you that you are an intelligent man. Don't be disheartened by our early fathers.

"Honestly we are thankful most of our Catholic brethren is quite naïve. Some of our early clergy wanted to keep the Latin language because the majority of our followers didn't understand it. Call it snob appeal. The first Vatican Council 1869-70 was conducted in Latin and a good number of bishops just pretended to understand. Twenty-four seminarians tried to translate it unsuccessfully. In 1962-65 they even tried a UN style translation system and still were unsuccessful. You might have noticed even legal documents, awards and diplomas are written in Latin just to appear more official. Pope John XXXIII allegedly displayed his displeasure at not using Latin by saying it is like dragging the through the gutter. As I am sure you gentlemen know he did acquiesce in regard to language and in Vatican II added the freedom to use the local language in the Mass.

"Hopefully the goodness we display outside these walls is what is visible to our flock. As I said, I have read some of these volumes you are reading. Some show the inner workings of the Vatican. Some put a nice, holy spin on our Church politics. The others seem to put an unholy light on our Papal workings. Unfortunately, I have to say, both are correct. There are some future saints in the Vatican and there are some. . ., well, you know what I mean. You might find it strange that here in Rome Sunday Mass is lightly attended. I suppose Father Thiel told you to wear money belts as you walk around the grounds. Pickpockets run rampant here. I guess just like Chicago you have to protect your belongings. Women do not leave their purses in the pew when going up for Communion. They may not be there when they return. You're smart enough to know there's good and bad everywhere."

"Peter," said William, "some of it just makes me angry. Rosalie hasn't read them but I have mentioned certain contents to her. Being a policeman's wife she hasn't been sheltered from the sins of the world but she, like I, assumed things in Rome were all holy and just. If some of what I have read is true, there is hypocrisy, pride, power struggles, cheating, lying and sex in these buildings. On the flight over here, I told Rosalie there is no way I would accept the nomination to be Pope. Today, I changed my mind. If I can say this without appearing too egotistical, I think God wants me to lead the Church. I am going to assume I am the recipient of a miracle and I am going to try to change..., well, not change, but modify the direction of our Church. Does that sound too pompous Peter?"

"No, I don't think so. I would love to see our Church get on a more virtuous and responsive path. I want the Roman Catholic Church to be more approachable. But here's the problem. The Catholic Church has had leadership difficulties throughout all its history. It would be a monumental task to change it. Are you the man to do it? At this point you are a very humble man. Will you stay that way? If you accomplish some great, spiritual feat, will you remain William, the simple man from Illinois? Don't forget, Satan is still prowling the world. I am very sure at this very moment he's making plans on how to attack you."

Pope William said, "I just assumed the Church, the Vatican, was rigid and completely righteous in its doings. I am finding out there was and are a lot of dilemmas and even sinners scattered all around."

"William," said Rosalie, "do you realize what you are undertaking?"

"Yes I do, Rosalie. I want to dive in and see what I can to. It's like politics at home. I've seen young men and women be elected to public office full of good ideas. They are enthusiastic and ready to take on the old establishment. Then I've seen them beat down and thwarted in their attempts. Then they too become the old establishment. I see these old Cardinals acting just like the old establishment in government. They don't want change. They want to protect their little kingdoms. It's a 'good ol' boys' mentality. God forbid any young Cardinal gets appointed. The Cardinals usually elect an elder Cardinal to be Pope. Then that Pope appoints other Cardinals thinking like he does. And so it goes, on and on.

"I remember reading what the late Cardinal Carlo Maria Martini wrote, 'The Church is tired... Our culture is aged, our churches are large, our religious houses empty, the Churches bureaucratic apparatus is growing and vestments pompous.' The Cardinal was a friend of Pope Francis. I read about him in the book *The Great Reformer* by Austen Ivereich."

Cardinal Whittier shook his head. "William, I sure want to be around to watch sparks fly. The Holy Spirit must feel you're the man to do it but be careful. Uneasy lies the head that wears the crown, to quote a phrase. And if I might add, and I don't want to scare you, past history has shown that some achievers have had untimely deaths."

"Bill!" said Rosalie.

Cardinal Whittier quickly added, "Times have changed, Rosalie. I just wanted to keep William's feet on earth."

William laughed. "Like times of old, I'll have a royal taster."

"You will have those fighting you tooth and nail, William. A word of advice, don't let a Cardinal or the press rush you into making a spontaneous or off the cuff answer to an enmeshing question. You will have to keep your wits about you. It's just like news reporters in the States. They will try to get you to answer trick questions before you get a chance to think it through and give a proper reply."

"I think I'd have an easier time of it if I was suddenly elected president," said William.

"Definitely. I think now I should leave you alone to write your speech. I got the impression you don't want Josip to write it."

"Right. What do you think of Father Thiel?"

"From what I've seen of him, I think he's an honest man. Do you still want to assign me to remain here in Rome?"

"Yes."

"Then I can work with him," said the Cardinal. "You will definitely need two or three more priests to be secretaries or aids. And if I may be so presumptuous, I'd like to have a couple of Cardinals to assist me."

"Okay. Just tell me who they are and I'll assign them."

Rosalie asked, "What about Sister Rose Williams?"

"I don't know her. You'd best ask Father Thiel."

"How odd. She has the same name as my husband. It must be a sign."

Cardinal Whittier smiled. "You believe in signs I see."

"Very much so," said William.

As the Cardinal walked to the door he said, "I look forward to hearing your speech tomorrow."

William walked over to Rosalie and put his arm around her. "Rosalie. What shall I say in my speech?

Should I begin expounding with all my thoughts about how I can improve our Church?"

Rosalie smiled, "Bill, you know better than that."

"I know. Just teasing," said Bill. "I keep having a difficult time taking myself seriously. I'm supposed to appear on that balcony and talk to several thousand people - no, millions. I'm supposed to say great things about what I'm going to do to help our followers get to heaven. I just cannot believe God wants me to be Jesus's vicar on Earth. I'm not even a priest."

Rosalie said, "It doesn't seem real to me either. I must say, though, the boys are having a ball. All they can talk about is soccer.

"I guess we'll just ride it out and see what happens."

William hugged Rosalie and said, "I love you Rosalie. Stick by me and keep me grounded."

"I will, Bill."

CHAPTER TWELVE

For the first time in modern history, a layman has been elected Pope. Close to a million people gathered at or near St. Peter's square. They are anticipating what the new leader's first words will be. Thanks to the media, over a billion are waiting to hear what this policeman nominated Pope has to say. They gathered themselves around the obelisk at the center of St. Peter's Square. The only one more nervous than Pope William is Cardinal Perez. Cardinal Whittier is a close third. All of the Cardinals of the Conclave have remained to hear the speech. The Vatican Press, as well as all the major networks, has set up their microphones and television cameras for this extremely rare event. The Cardinals are laying odds as to the reception the audience will give William. It could be anything from cheers to silence to boos. The fact that he is not Italian is also adding to the suspense.

Cardinal Perez inched closer to Pope William and said, "Did you have any trouble reading my speech this morning?"

"No," said William.

"Good. Cardinal Santo will translate it to Italian as you speak. He has his own copy."

"Good," said William.

Suddenly Cardinal Perez got even more nervous. "You will read my speech William?"

"I've read your speech several times, Josip," said the new Pope. "I can see you've put a lot of thought into it."

As they prepared to open the curtain and move out on the balcony, Cardinal Perez positioned himself even closer to William.

Pope William said, "I'd like Cardinal Whittier on my right and Cardinals Evans and Larenzo nearby on my left." These were the two Cardinals Cardinal Whittier requested to aid him.

"Definitely not!" exclaimed Cardinal Perez.

"Please step back, Josip," said William in a firm voice.

"I will not!" said Cardinal Perez in a louder voice.

Pope William said to two of the Swiss guards, "Would you help the Cardinal move to the rear."

A couple of other Cardinals said to Cardinal Perez, "You're making a scene, Josip. Move out of the way."

"You can't do this!" said Cardinal Perez.

"I just did. Rosalie, you should stand just slightly ahead of me, next to Cardinal Whittier."

"I'm scared," said Rosalie.

"I am too, dear."

As the group moved out to the balcony, there was an awkward silence. Pope William became aware of a sea of people. He could not believe the signs, flags and banners scattered throughout the crowd. Then someone started clapping and soon more followed. Then there was more and soon it turned into a fairly loud cheer.

"Wave," said Cardinal Whittier.

Pope William's wave started quite feebly but as his confidence grew, so did his wave.

"You wave too, Rosalie," said Cardinal Whittier. The Cardinal whispered to William, "This reminds me of our president and first lady greeting the crowd in Washington."

"That's right," said William. "You're a U. S. citizen, aren't you?"

"Born in Iowa."

"Well, here goes." Pope William took the microphone. William took out a sheet of paper with his short speech written on it.

"William!" screamed Josip. "You must give the speech I wrote for you! I will not allow you to do otherwise."

Cardinal Salas said, "As we say in Colorado, Josip. You must ride the bronc you brought to the rodeo. Evidently we elected William as our Pope. Let's ride it out and see where it leads us."

Cardinal Perez began trying to pull away from the Swiss guards but they held fast, moving him farther to the rear of the room.

"Cardinal Larenzo, are you ready to translate? I will pause after each sentence."

The Cardinal said, "Ready."

"Ladies and gentlemen." William paused. "I hesitate to say 'My brethren in Christ' as other Popes have said. That would be too presumptuous. I also hesitate to say I am your Pope. Just as you, I do not understand how or why I am standing on this hallowed balcony addressing you. I hope Cardinal Larenzo's translating doesn't make my speech too awkward.

"I, and the Cardinals, have discussed many times in the last few days just how it is I am here. We have repeated the obvious many, many times. The most apparent scenarios are this: the Holy Spirit has performed a miracle, Satan has performed a tremendously evil deed, some trickster has performed a horribly foul endeavor, or, we just have no answer. So, here is what I am going to do. First, I am going to explain just who I am. Then, with the help of Cardinal Whittier, a highly respected Cardinal from my home state of Illinois, I will try to explain what I will try to do as Pope, or what I will not try to do as Pope.

"I am – or was - a 51 year old policeman from Peoria, Illinois in the United States. I was born in Germany. My wife Rosalie was born here in Italy." I small cheer rose from the crowd. "I have two sons, Charles eighteen and David fifteen. My wife is quickly becoming at ease again with the Italian language and I am working to become fluent again in German.

"Most Catholics agree our Church is faltering. Today there are many Catholics giving lip service by saying they are Catholics, but are not practicing the Faith. In the last few days I have thought of that and wondered what a Pope could do to change that fact. Here is one of my humble thoughts. Pray for me. All priests, bishops, Cardinals and Popes have said the words of 'Pray for me'. I hesitate to say pray for me because I don't feel I deserve your prayers. Who am I to ask for your prayers? I am only a policeman from the United States. I am not highly educated. I have not studied in a religious facility. I am not ordained and do not intend to be. Why should you pray for me? I suppose the answer is because somehow I was elected as your leader.

"Let's first assume God has picked me to be Pope. There must be something in my thoughts that God wants me to expound upon. I have no idea what it could be but hopefully God will place the inspiration on my lips. Yes, Pray for me. Like most laypeople, I never prayed all that much. Truthfully, I prayed the most when the plane hit turbulence on the flight over here. I feel hypocritical asking you to pray for me. But, if I am truly to be Pope, I will do my best to do the proper thing. I will try to put common sense back into our Faith."

At the last sentence, Cardinal Perez tried to violently shake loose from the arms of the Swiss Guards. It was to no avail.

"Second, let's assume this is the work of Satan. Cardinal Perez has hired an extremely efficient private detective to ascertain if this is the work of the devil or most probably a hoax. If he can disprove that this is a miracle, I will immediately resign as Pope. It is for this reason I will move most cautiously and slowly with any edict I proclaim. I will confer most judiciously with all Canon Lawyers at my disposal. I have asked Cardinal Whittier to remain here in Rome to advise me as to how to go about getting their advice and consul.

"I believe there are challenges facing our Church. I will address them later after I consult with our Cardinals and bishops. I will start with the most simple and progress to the most serious. I have begun to read several volumes of Vatican books. It is a sort of crash course on the good works of the Vatican over the centuries. But I have also read some of the not so good works. For instance; corrupt Papal politics, malevolent secrets, hidden diaries, criminal abuses, immoral behaviors and corruption and just plain sins." A reserved cheer arose from the crowd. "I certainly realize these writers surely put their spin on their writings. But as I have said, I also read several volumes of the good side of the Vatican. Yes, those writers put their spin on their writings, too. Already several staff members have tried to get my ear. That happens anytime there is someone who feels slighted by someone in higher authority. In my occupation as a policeman, I know how it works.

"So, yes. I am asking you to pray for me. Let me be most assuredly transparent. Be patient with me as I learn the ropes. I can assure you, I will not take the Church backward. I will try to take Holy Mother the Church forward into modern times with Jesus Christ as our leader." A small cheer again rose from the crowd.

Cardinal Whittier whispered in William's ear. "Tell them your chosen name."

"Oh, I have chosen to be Pope William." Again, there was a controlled applause but at least it was a positive response.

"Cardinal Whittier will give you a Blessing. I will explain why I can't give a Papal Blessing.

"Friends. I am not an ordained bishop or priest. I cannot give a blessing. For the time being, we will dispense with a Vatican Blessing. It will be given by Cardinal Whittier. I am sure there will be other changes in procedures. We are in a new era for our Church. I hope God will guide us to improved relations with our faithful, other Christian denominations, those who are agnostics or atheists and those who are our antagonists. Thank you."

Again a reserved applause rose from the crowd. It was obvious some in the audience applauded and some did not.

Cardinal Whittier came to the front of the balcony and gave the large audience his blessing. As they turned to leave he then turned to Pope William, "Your holiness, we must talk."

"I know. Let's do it now."

"Fine. In your office?"

"Yes."

As the crowd began dispersing, Pope William gave the Swiss Guards permission to release Cardinal Perez.

A very angry Cardinal Perez said, "You will deplore the day you defied me." He then turned and walked away. "Francisco, Giovani, come with me."

Cardinal Francisco Santo seemed to hesitate. "Francisco! I said come with me!"

"I think not," said Francisco.

"Are you going to follow this heathen?"

Francisco looked the other way and didn't answer.

"How about you, Karl?"

Cardinal Stanlove answered, "I am going to give the Pope some time. I am going to see what develops.

As Cardinal Perez approached the door, he turned and faced the new Pope. With terse and deliberate wording he said, "I can assure you that John Paul's reign of 33 days will seem like an eternity compared to the length of your reign, Pope William." The Cardinal almost hissed the words, 'Pope William'.

"What is wrong with you, Josip?" said Cardinal Whittier. "We must assume this is the work of the Holy Spirit until proven otherwise."

"Never!" said Josip. "With God as my witness, never!" Then he turned to Cardinals Paulo and Peligrini. "Will you come with me?"

The two Cardinals looked at each other and reluctantly agreed. "For the moment, Josip, we will listen to what you have to say."

Pope William, Cardinals Whittier, Larenzo and Evans went to the new Pope's office and seated themselves near a large crucifix.

Pope William said, "Peter. I need to know whom to trust. I know most of your time as Cardinal has been in the United States but do you have any feel regarding trustworthy people here in Rome? I am reading my library books as quickly as I can. The corruption here seems so prevalent."

"William," said Peter. "There is corruption but it is not as widespread as it may seem. There is a kind of human frailty that seems to occur in any secret society. Unfortunately the Vatican is a very secret society. What is even more unfortunate, the Vatican wants to remain that way. The frailty is the fact that secret societies seem to feel they are above the rules. In other words, they begin to feel they are above the law."

"Tell me something I don't know," said William. "I've seen it first hand in my own police department. I've seen good men – and women - turn away from good."

"So William, it has happened in the past, it is happening now and will continue to happen in the future. Believe me, William, you are not immune although your humility will shield you somewhat."

"You will have to help me, Peter. I found myself feeling somewhat arrogant and haughty when I told the Swiss Guards to restrain Josip. I am already a sinner; my first sin as Pope."

Cardinal Whittier said, "It is a saying, 'the higher the position in the Church, the easier and farther it is to fall'."

"Peter, can you find people I can trust?"

"Starting with me?"

"Yes," said William. "I have to start with you and of course Cardinals Anthony Larenzo and Ronald Evans."

"Thank you. I will start tomorrow," Cardinal Whittier said. "I will prepare a list of Cardinals, bishop, priests, attendants, and even cooks, servants and maids. I know you will even want to know some of the Swiss Guards and whom to trust. You may even want to work out in the gym with some of them. That will endear you to them greatly. The same goes for bishops, priests and staff. I can see you have an outgoing manner about you. That will help you, too. Also Rosalie will need to know which nuns can be trusted and that will take time. I don't mean to infer these people are thieves; you just need to know who can be trusted to not gossip. I've asked Anthony and Larenzo to help me."

William said, "I understand."

The Cardinal added, "Now keep this in mind. I've lived in Chicago most of my life. I know something of most of the Cardinals but there are some I've never met. We meet every five or so years, unless of course there is an election for a new pope. Actually, only forty or so Cardinals live at the Vatican. What this means is I know even less about the priests, bishops and other religious that live here. I'll talk to Cardinal Reardon. He lives here and we've worked together before."

"Thank you, Peter."

"I'll be leaving for Peoria soon. I'll meet you and Rosalie at the airport when you get there."

Rosalie said, "I told the boys you would pick them up and bring them to the airport."

"Fine. I am looking forward to meeting them," Cardinal Whittier said.

"I just hope they'll be properly dressed to meet you."

"Rosalie," said William. "Give the boys some credit." To the Cardinal he said, "Don't forget my list."

"I'm mentally making a list now."

"Cardinal," said Pope William. "do you think the public will truly accept me?"

"We're in God's hands."

"Okay," replied the worried young pope.

CHAPTER THIRTEEN

Cardinal Perez scheduled his own little meeting with Cardinals Signorelli, Paulo and Peligrini for Monday morning.

The Cardinal stood in front of Cardinals Signorelli, Paulo and Peligrini. He then began pacing back and forth in front of them. "Gentlemen, we have come upon evil times. I don't know how it happened. My detective friend hasn't visited me as of yet. I will contact him again tomorrow and tell him it's most urgent we meet. Detective Candelo is very thorough and will soon give us the information we need to force this imposter Pope to resign."

"Are you sure?"

"Yes," said Josip. "We have a good thing going here and I'll not let some ignorant cop ruin it. Gentlemen, I intend to be Pope, no matter what. I assure you it'll be soon."

The Cardinals glanced at each other and then looked at Josip. "Josip, are you so sure this isn't a miracle?"

"Damn it!" screamed Josip. "I will be Pope! Our Church has been retreating for the last 70 years. Women don't wear head dress in church any more. There are girl altar servers and women reading from the pulpit. Women are even giving out Holy Communion. It's the work of the devil. This man is Satan in the flesh. I want women cleaning the altar, ironing our vestments, dusting the pews and cleaning toilets. That's all!" Josip was still yelling.

There was a knock at the door. "Yes! Who is it?"

A handsome, young man appeared at the door. "Josip, do you want to see me tonight?"

"No!" Cardinal Perez yelled. "Go away."

Cardinals Paulo and Peligrini stood up and headed toward the door. "Josip, I will not listen to your ranting and raving. Vincent and I are leaving."

"Go! Don't come crying to me when he – God forbid - wants to ordain a woman. It'll be the end of the Roman Catholic Church." Then, in a quieter tone, Josip said, "God will see that he dies before any sacrilegious events happen. Have you forgotten? The Holy Spirit protects us from any pope preaching or proclaiming a false doctrine. It's been said down through the ages if a pope would declare an edict that there are only nine commandments or some such statement the Holy Spirit would remove him from the living."

"We don't know if that's true, Josip," said Cardinal Paulo. "It's probably just a fable."

"I don't care. I have a feeling our young cop is already near death and the Spirit may be moving to make me his finger of death."

Cardinal Peligrini said, "Josip Perez! What are you saying?"

"Go! Get out!"

Only Cardinal Signorelli remained. "Josip, be careful. I say again. This just may be a miracle."

Refusing to fly in the Papal aircraft, the Pope's commercial aircraft approached the Peoria airport.

"Ladies and gentlemen, we will be landing at General Wayne A Downing Peoria airport in twenty minutes. Please see that your seat backs and tray tables are up and fully locked. The local time is seven minutes past six in the morning."

Rosalie said, "William, you have been reading those books all night. Did you get any sleep?"

"No. There is so much to learn about the Vatican. I hope I can sound half way intelligent if anybody asks me a question. You know? I am formulating several ideas to modernize the Church. I wonder if the Holy Spirit is placing these ideas in my mind, or is it that I am just thinking of things that drive me nuts."

"Bill, just be careful," said Rosalie. "Don't do anything too preposterous. I feel presumptuous even saying this but if you are really going to be Pope – I guess I should say you are the Pope – you should think of how history will regard you. I glanced at one of your pope books. Some of the popes were not looked upon too kindly."

"I know, Rosalie. That does worry me. I am trusting Cardinal Whittier to help me. He got back to Peoria yesterday and is supposed to meet us at the airport. I guess I've caused him some distress also. He has a lot of arrangements to make here in order for him to relocate to Rome. The diocese will take over our home and other expenses we have. They have to make arrangements for you and the boys if I should be so unfortunate to die. I can't will anything to you that belong to the Church. I guess I am just a non-person when it comes to material wealth. I own nothing. There will be nothing to inherit except my police retirement funds."

"Are the boys going to meet us at the airport?"

William answered, "Yeah, they're supposed to. Cardinal Whittier said he'd bring them. They sure sounded excited. I wonder if anybody else will be there from our parish?"

A flight attendant approached William, "Well, your Holiness," she said. "It looks like our little Peoria airport is having its largest crowd around it since the last president visited us."

"What? It was supposed to be kept quiet. I guess the news leaked."

"Even at this early hour there could be over a million people gathered here. We've never had a U. S. citizen named Pope, especially from Peoria. I happen to be Catholic too, although I don't practice my faith too much. Maybe you'll change that."

"I don't think I can change that," said William. "You'll have to do that."

Pope William sat up in his seat, looking out his window. The plane was still too high to see through the clouds. William said, "What do you mean?"

"Like I said," the attendant continued, "we don't often get notables visiting Peoria, and you are quite a notable. I may even try to go to one of your Masses."

"Oh," said William, "I can't say a Mass."

"Why not?"

"It's complicated," said William. "It'll be explained later. But I can't believe it. A crowd you say?"

"It sure is. Traffic is backed up for miles, even at this early hour. Your arrival has created a traffic jam. Why didn't you fly Air Alitalia like other Popes?"

William continued looking out the window. "I just felt no need for such an expense. It'd be such a waste of money better spent elsewhere."

"Bill," said Rosalie. "I still cannot believe what is happening."

"I can't either. Cardinal Whittier said a lot of saints had trouble believing God was performing a miracle through them. I can't believe God is working a miracle through me, a cop. And, I surely don't believe I am a saint."

"I know, Bill," said Rosalie. "Sometimes I want to laugh when I think of you as a saint and then I want to shy away from you. Should I pray to you? Should I call you St. William? Maybe they'll make a little, plastic statue of you."

"Rosalie, please be serious. I don't know where this will lead us. Sometimes I actually hope it turns out to be a trick. A hoax. I didn't do it but I wouldn't mind a bit if Cardinal Perez's detective finds out someone is playing a trick on the Vatican. Then I could go back to being a dumb cop."

"Bill, you were never a dumb cop. You were always the most conscientious policeman I ever knew."

"Rosalie, you have to keep me well grounded."

"I'll try, Bill. I'll try."

CHAPTER FOURTEEN

Cardinal Perez's private secretary entered his office. "Your eminence, there is a Mr. Candelo here to see you. He said he has an appointment."

"Yes he does. Send him in."

Father Pate opened the office door and motioned for Mr. Candelo to enter.

Edwardo Candelo was tall, robust, broad shouldered man about six feet four. He wore a black, pin stripped suit, which bulged with his muscles. His black, shiny shoes squeaked as he walked.

Cardinal Perez almost jumped up from his chair, at least as much as an overweight man could jump, his outstretched hand reaching to shake the detective's large, hairy hand. "Come in, Edwardo. Come in," he said.

With a gravelly voice he said, "Hello, Mr. Perez. I really am at a loss wondering why one of you holy guys would want to see me." He stuck out a massive hand to shake with the cardinal.

"I'll quickly explain," said the Cardinal. "As you have probably heard our latest Pope has been elected by some very unusual means. You have heard, haven't you?"

"Yeah. Some kind of magic."

"Exactly, some kind of magic." Even though the Cardinal and the detective were most likely the same weight, the detective's weight was distributed quite differently. As he moved, the detective's arms filled out his suit coat's sleeves quite well and the buttons on his suit coat were straining to keep his chest caged. As for comparison, it had been forty years since Cardinal Perez has seen his toes. The Cardinal stood up for emphasis. "I want you to find out how this magic could have been done. None of the

Cardinals voted for the man and yet his name appeared on four different voting procedures. I am going to give you a carte blanc pass to allow you to go anywhere on Vatican grounds. With this pass no one will challenge you or prohibit you from going anywhere you desire at any time of the day. Here are several other passes you can use for any of your associates as needed."

"Wow," said the detective. "You're serious."

"Deadly serious. Edwardo, are you Catholic?"

"No. Not since my Baptism. Why do you ask?"

Cardinal Perez said, "Edwardo, the Pope is the supreme ruler of our Catholic Church. He must be a very holy man, brought up through the ranks as you say. There is no way an unknown man – a policeman – can be elected Pope. It just can't happen. Some way, somehow a trick was perpetrated on the Conclave. I will reward you handsomely for discovering out how this could be achieved. It must also be executed with dispatch. This man could set back our Church hundreds of years. He may even devastate it."

"Okay, okay," the big man said. "What do I have to work with?"

"Here. I have one hundred ballots from the last three elections. Twenty are from the second election, forty are from the third election and about forty are from the last election. You'll notice the last groups are even signed."

"Are they the Cardinals actual signatures?" asked Mr. Candelo.

"Yes because I personally asked each of those Cardinals if that was their signature. They swore on the Holy Bible that it was their signatures but they did not write that man's name."

"Interesting."

Cardinal Perez said, "Can you do this task?"

"Yeah, I have a several chemists who work with me on a lot of cases. They are not cheap, though."

"That's not a ..."

Mr. Candelo interrupted, "Mr. Perez. Let me state a fact here. You are not going to reward me. You're going to pay me and pay me handsomely. I will expect a large advance and an even larger final payment."

"That is not a problem," said the Cardinal.

"I like the sound of that," said Edwardo smiling. "First let me see the ballots. Then we'll review exactly what you want me to do and then we'll discuss payment."

The Cardinal handed Mr. Candelo a large, brown envelope. The detective opened the envelope and looked at a few ballots. "So, you want me to tell you how this could be done, right?"

"Exactly."

"No problem. How long do I have?"

"The sooner the better," said the Cardinal. "Two to three months."

"My chemists are located in the States."

"I don't care if they are on the moon. Just do it."

"Okay, let's discuss my reward as you called it. Let's make it a $5,000.00 retainer, then $15,000.00 upon completion. Naturally I will add expenses to that and any other incidentals. Lastly, sometimes I get into trouble with the local law. I will expect you to bail me out, pay fines and lawyer fees. I'm assuming I will complete the task in three months. If it takes longer, I'll add $5,000.00 a month. Of course I want it in Uncle Sam's currency."

Cardinal Perez was momentarily stunned but quickly salvaged his composure. "That's a quite a large sum. Am I your only client?"

"That's none of your business but I have a lot of employees."

Cardinal Perez sat with his hands folded on his desk.

"Cash in unmarked bills," added Mr. Candelo. "Is that a problem?"

Recovering the Cardinal spoke, "There should be no trouble with any laws. There is nothing illegal about what you're going to do."

"Maybe and maybe not. Tomorrow I'll bring a contract with all that I've said included. You and two witnesses will sign it. Understood?"

"Two witnesses?"

"Yeah. Another problem?"

"You're telling me chemists are that expensive?"

"It's not just chemists. I told you I have a fair amount of employees. Take it or leave it. Don't forget. There will be some lack of discretion regarding my movements. You're paying for that, too."

"I told you there will be no need to hide you actions."

"You mean you don't care who knows you're paying me $20,000.00 or more in cash? Where are you getting that much money? That's a lot of change from your little collection baskets."

The Cardinal hadn't thought of that little point. "Three months?"

"Yeah. Deal?"

"It'll take me three days to get that much cash."

"No problem. Don't forget the witnesses. And don't even think about reneging on the final payment."

"Good day," said the Cardinal.

"See ya."

As Mr. Candelo left, the Cardinal called his secretary in. "Georgio, get Cardinal Santo and Signorelli for me. I know they are still in the Vatican."

Cardinal Perez still felt he was doing the necessary thing but getting that much cash bothered him. He was already thinking of ways to reneging on the final payment. It was a large sum of cash for Josip to acquire in such a short time, and it had to be in U S currency. He also needed two witnesses. His secretary, Georgio would serve as one and hopefully Cardinal Signorelli would serve as the other.

Cardinal Perez had a slush fund he had been building over the years but he hated to delve into it. He also had a prostitute he had used before to help influence judgments. Josip cared little for the female persuasion but he never hesitated to use their sway.

Pope William and Rosalie headed down the jetway. As predicted by the airline attendant, there was a hoard of people as well as TV camera men and women lined up along the hallway. Bill saw Cardinal Whittier and the boys in the front of the mass of people. Behind the Cardinal a flock of reporters began asking questions. William was able to avoid them for the moment. He couldn't believe the people holding out their hands, asking William to forgive them. Also there were several handicapped people yelling for William to cure them. It was almost disgusting. It reminded him of some of the Bible scenes depicting Jesus surrounded by lame and diseased people.

The new Pope moved to get to the Cardinal. "Peter, am I glad to see you. What's going on?"

"You, your Holiness, are quite a celebrity. "

"Really?" said William. "I can't believe it. I'm not even wearing religious garb. I left Peoria a nobody and now everybody wants to see me and ask ridiculous questions. They even want me to cure them."

"I know, William," said the Cardinal. "They know the story behind your election. I've had to answer a few questions already. The first was who will you name as Cardinal for our diocese. Then they wanted to know what your feelings are on abortion, stem cell therapy and how you will treat gays and lesbians."

"I expected that. You'll have to give me some input on some of those problems. I guess we'll have to work on other issues, too."

Rosalie and Bill rushed to see their sons. They gave each other big hugs, Rosalie shedding a tear. "I missed you guys. It looks like you dressed yourselves appropriately."

"Thanks, Mom. Hey! Father Johnston even got us passports. I guess we're going to Rome. Ricky and Bob can't believe it. Sherry even shed a tear." These children were classmates of David and Charles.

Cardinal Whittier asked, "Do you want to give an interview now or later?"

"Peter, I don't want to appear unapproachable but I am beat. Rosalie is too. It's been a long flight. Then again, maybe I should give a short interview."

"That would be great. It would be a great commencement of an open and transparent reign."

"I guess."

"William," said Cardinal Whittier, "I am really excited. I think this will be an exhilarating and illuminating time for our Church. This could actually be a miracle transpired by the Holy Spirit. Oh, and Father Johnston said to bring you over to the rectory no matter what time you got in."

"Peter, I hope you are correct in assuming the Holy Spirit managed my election. I hope He stays close by to help me."

"I'm sure He is right next to you."

Pope William handled several questions thrown at him by the press and television channels. The strangest of all was, "Your Holiness. Are you going to wear a gun?"

"I'll have the Swiss Guards surrounding me."

Another question, "Your Holiness, when can you and your wife have sex?"

"After dark," was the Popes answer.

"Holy Father, my son wants to be a priest at the Vatican," asked a woman. "Would you see he gets in?"

"Holy Father," said Pope William. "Am I really the Holy Father?"

"You the man," said Cardinal Whittier.

With that, he and Rosalie headed to the Cardinal's vehicle and to their home – which was soon to become a part of St. Sabina Church. Some form of lease would be arranged. The Pope and Rosalie still had to decide what would go to Rome and what would be placed in storage. Their boys talked incessantly about soccer, and of course, pizza.

CHAPTER FIFTEEN

After two weeks of arranging their affairs, the Pope, his family and Cardinal Whittier were on their way back to Rome. Once again they flew commercial. William could tell Cardinal Whittier was not accustomed to flying coach.

"I can guarantee you, William," said Cardinal Whittier, "the next time you fly, you will be on Air Alitalia with a large entourage. "

David asked, "Father, I heard Dad say some of the Swiss Guards wear plainclothes and are armed. Is that true?"

Pope William said, "David, you will call him 'Your Eminence'."

"Oh," said David.

Cardinal Whittier said, "David, you can call me Peter. Yes we have plainclothes guards and they are armed."

In a hushed tone, in order not to be heard by other passengers, Pope William said, "Peter, how will I issue my edicts, that is, if I dare to issue any? Who will censure me or who will judge my proclamations?"

"William, you will have a horde of people to judge you. The Cardinals, archbishops, bishops, priests, seminarians and even cooks and janitors will gladly give advice. To co-ordinate things between you and representatives of the Church, you will have the Synod of Bishops established in 1965 by Pope Paul VI. Seriously, though, the College of Cardinals, College of Bishops and Roman Curia will always be at your shoulder to tell you what you can do and can't do."

"Okay. Then who has the last word?"

"The Pope has the last word. It's you, your Holiness. As they say in Chicago, 'You' the man'."

"Wow."

"Canon 331 says you possess full, supreme, immediate and universal ordinary power to govern the Catholic Church. The Code of Canon Law was instigated by Pope Pius X around the early nineteen hundreds. No one can appeal a papal decision. Canon 1372 says even an attempt to appeal to an ecumenical council is forbidden. Actually, Canon 1417 says that a baptized Catholic has the right to appeal directly to Rome and to the Pope. Sometimes this is called *the appeal to Ceasar*."

Cardinal Whittier added, "It's like politics; some will love you, some will only like you, some won't care, some will dislike you and some will hate you. There will be those that will plan for your demise and some will just start their own religious denomination. You're a novice here. I'll try to help you negotiate the bureaucracy as best I can. But remember, I was located in the States. I am not greatly experienced in Vatican styles of administration. You'll have to appoint someone as Secretary of State. He will be your liaison between you and all other offices."

"How about you, Peter?"

"Dear God. I guess I should have expected that. Let me think about it, William."

"I need you, Peter," said the Pope. "What about languages? I have already received many letters and communiques in other languages. What should I do?"

"Don't worry. They will all go through one of the language desks. I will then bring them to you. You will have to inform your friends to send any personal communications to your secretary. That will be one of the priests I will recommend. "

Cardinal Whittier assured the boys they wouldn't have to wear altar boy vestments. He also assured them they wouldn't have to pray twenty-four seven. "Maybe just before meals," he added.

Cardinal Whittier had briefed the Pope on matters of importance awaiting him. It was most overwhelming. William was trying to sort out what was most important and what to do first. Due to the late hour the crowd at the airport in Rome was not as large as the throngs in Peoria and William was glad. As before, television and press personnel were mixed in with the people asking a plethora of questions. William tried to answer as best he could while still walking to his limousine. Father Thiel was there to greet him. They rode to the Vatican in silence.

Charles and David fell asleep even though they said they couldn't wait to see the city of Rome. It was Monday, two A M local time.

The next morning Cardinal Whittier met the new Pope. "Well, your Holiness, this is the first day of your tenure as Pope. What are your plans for the day?"

"I guess I have to get my family situated. The boys are in a rush to see all of Vatican City and Rosalie wants to talk to Sister Rose Williams about the furnishings of the Papal apartment. I guess you, Peter, will lead me to my first appointment."

"I've talked to several of the Cardinals and." Peter paused, "William, you have quite a fight coming up with Cardinal Perez and some of his companions. He is trying very hard to recruit as many Cardinals, bishops, priests and anybody that'll listen to his opinion regarding you as Pope. He's determined to get you to resign."

"Can he force me to resign?"

"No," said the Cardinal. "Only you can make that decision. In truth, unless a Pope dies there is no way for a Pope to be removed unless he resigns. We've had some mentally ill Popes over the centuries but no way exists to remove them. I hate to say this but it seems some were poisoned. I'm sure you've read that in your readings."

William said, "I have and I found it hard to believe. Is our history that tainted?"

"I'm afraid so. In the early Church a thorough autopsy wasn't possible and even now no autopsy is allowed."

William said, "That's strange, and scary."

"But Josip can make it very uncomfortable for you. He'll fight any decision you make. He wants to take the Church back sixty or seventy years. William, he is very afraid of women and does not want them in the Church hierarchy. I don't know why."

William went to a window of his apartment. "Peter, that is one thing that has really bothered me about the Catholic Church. Why have we always been so against women? Why do we treat them as property as the ancient Muslims or Arabs did, and some cases still do?"

Cardinal Whittier appeared thoughtful. "William, on that point, be careful. The treatment of women isn't just the result of 2000 years of culture but actually 20,000 years of defining the woman's role on Earth. In the days of the caveman the man hunted and the woman had babies. We're not that bad but... Avoid any great and sudden changes of the woman's responsibility in the Church."

"Peter, I feel God wants me to do something on that subject. But don't worry. I'll do nothing drastic without your input."

"Fair enough," said the Cardinal.

"Were there any non-cardinals other than me elected?" asked Willian.

"Yes, Urban VI in 1378. He appointed twenty-nine Cardinals and they quickly abandoned him. He was one of the Popes allegedly poisoned"

"First thing," said the Pope, "What exactly is the Holy See?"

"The word Holy See comes from the Latin word Santa Sedes. It means Holy Seat. It is covered under Canon 331. I guess the best way to explain it is that it is a composite of the jurisdiction, authority and sovereignty vested in you, the Pope. The Holy See consists of advisors to direct the Roman Catholic Church around the world and the legal central government of the Church. It can send and receive diplomatic representatives to 179 nations. Vatican City does not send or receive diplomatic representatives. The Holy See acts on its behalf on international affairs. In 1939, Pope Pius XII established the unicameral Pontifical Commission consisting of seven Cardinals for five year terms. Any laws passed by the Commission must still be approved by you. It still must pass through the Secretariat of State before being published and taking effect.

"You will have to appoint a President of the Pontifical Commission of the Vatican State. You will delegate executive authority to the President who will serve a five year term. You can remove him at any time. The president will report all important issues to the Secretary of State. That is a brief explanation of the Executive branch. It is similar to the Legislation branch. Laws and policies passed by the Commission must be approved by you and published in the Italian language *Acta Apostolicae.*

"We also have a seldom used judiciary and penal system. Major crimes are handled by the Italian authorities. They handle any imprisonments with the Vatican covering the costs."

"Wow," said an astounded Pope William. "I don't think I can remember all of that. What about it? Can I appoint you as my Secretary of State?"

"It's your choice, William."

"Peter, am I really in charge? I don't want to sound too authoritative but can I make new rules? I don't mean doctrine but just changes in day to day policy. What I mean is I don't want to change anything about the Ten Commandments. I wouldn't dare, but there have been changes in how long we have to fast before receiving communion, holy days and eating meat on Fridays."

"Those are just changes in interpretations made by different popes," said Cardinal Whittier. "Even Bible interpretations have changed many times over the years. A pope can do that but there will always be some resistance from someone somewhere. Some changes were too radical and resulted in priests, bishops or archbishops breaking away. I fear some of the changes I see coming from your papacy will result in – I hate to say it – schisms."

Pope William appeared thoughtful. "From what I have read our Church has had schisms or breakaways throughout its history. Peter, I am going to assume God really wants me to make our Church a contemporary Church. Unless Cardinal Perez can uncover some plot in my being elected I am going to pursue my feelings. I am going to assume God wants me to make changes. Not doctrine changes but just minor changes of what previous popes or Cardinals have done. Peter, my favorite verse comes from Matthew 22:39. When Jesus was asked 'Which is the greatest of the commandments?' He replied 'You shall love the Lord your God with all you heart, with all soul, and with all your mind.' This is the greatest and first commandment. And the second is like it: 'You shall love your neighbor as yourself.' I don't see that being practiced by many of our Church leaders."

"William, you will have to call an Ecumenical Council as stated in Canon Law."

"Can they overrule me?"

"No, the council is not superior to the Pope and it cannot judge you or impeach you. I have to add, in church history these precepts have been violated. I guess you can say that except for the Ten Commandments, our Church is quite fluid."

Pope William added, "I think what my ideas boil down to is I don't like some of our man-made rules. I believe these rules to be the bones of contention that many fallen away Catholics harbor. I also feel the New Testament is more accurate than the Old Testament. I feel there is a lot of folk lore in the Old Testament."

"Interesting," was all Cardinal Whittier could say.

"Okay. I want to first address Confession. I am sure you know the confessional is used more as a broom closet then a place for reconciliation. I would like to have a meeting of some Cardinals and Bishops sympathetic to changes in the manner of Confession. I feel it is being conducted in the wrong way. I've managed several organizations in my parish and confession is one of the things driving Catholics away from the Church. The congregation doesn't participate. Before Christmas and Easter we have more priests available for confession than sinners. And I am sure you know the alleged story that confession was instigated in Ireland in the eighteenth or nineteenth century. The clergy wanted to know the secrets of the royalty. Then there's celibacy and the erroneous perception of annulment by Catholics and non-Catholics alike. Last, the misconception non-Catholics have about our praying to saints. We don't pray to saints, we ask them to intercede to our heavenly Father for us."

"I think I can guess what you're going to say."

"Let's start with Reconciliation," continued William. "I'm sure all of your cardinal brethren have read John Cornwell's book *'The Dark Box: A Secret History of Confession.* While not completely thorough, it gives a good first glance at the problems of the confessional. Read what Dr. Joseph Mizzi says about the Council of Trent, Session 14, Canon 6. It states, 'But, as regards the minister of the sacrament (Penance), the holy Synod declares all these doctrines to be false, and utterly alien from the truth of the Gospel, which perniciously extend the ministry of the keys to any other server besides bishops and priests; imagining, contrary to the institution of the sacrament.' There's nothing there about a dark box, just that only a priest or bishop can forgive sins. I think confession in that little box is archaic and threatening. I've gone to confession to some bad priests and good priests. I don't like the procedure of going into that room or closet and whispering my sins. Some priests – and I mean just a few – seem to get their jollies listening to peoples' sins, especially women's sins. I guess I shouldn't use that word but you know what I mean. At least the women maltreated by those priests have come forward. Hopefully the priests committing those crimes have left the Church.

"I am sure you all know the facts. If you don't remember your studies, I'll refresh you. During the seventh century Irish missionaries, inspired by some Eastern monastic traditions, brought the private practice of secret confessions. This also brought about the required frequency of confession for venial as well as grave sins. Read again your Catechism of the Catholic Church, paragraph 1447. It seems the Church dares us to even suggest that secret confession to a priest was not observed from the time of Christ. It states 'Wherefore, whereas the secret sacramental confession, which was in use from the beginning in holy Church, and is still also in use,...' This statement is false. It was not in use in the beginning of the Church."

"Adding to the dangers of frustrated priest having intimate contact to children, Pope Pius X decreed that confession should begin at age seven. No one else need by present. And the early Church dealt quite severely with sin. They were cast out of the Church, demanding a period of public penance before they could be readmitted. When they repented, they confessed directly to God."

Cardinal Whittier said, "How do you know that?"

"Don't act like you don't know anything about it, Peter. It's some more of those crimes hidden by the Vatican. Do you delete those unpleasant actualities from your memory?"

Cardinal Whittier seemed thoughtful. "There's no need to make that public."

"Peter!" said William, "Here we go again hiding our dirty laundry. Fortunately most Catholics do not have to delve deeply into Church history like I have had to in recent months. I've just procured another book from the Vatican library; 'The Entity' by Eric Frattini. I can't wait to read it. Have your read it?"

"Yes. We can discuss it sometime in the future." William could tell the cardinal wasn't in the mood to talk about the book.

"No! Now."

"Fine. Let me say this about expose books. The Catholic Church has gone through a violent and tumultuous past. There will always be writers seeking something shocking about our past. It's like that movie *Conspiracy Theory* or whatever it was called. Some news people always like to find some secret. They have to sell newspapers or TV time. They look for insiders with secrets to sell. They look for spies. Any big organization – and the Catholic Church is a big organization – has secrets and the Church has many."

William said, "But is that what Christ wanted? I always thought He wanted peace and love. He wanted openness."

"William, you're forgetting humans, and their many faults, are running the Church. Yes, the early Popes were like kings or military leaders with armies under their command. They fought battles. They fought the Protestant reformers. There were all kinds of secret and not so secret organizations. There were the Crusades, the Inquisitions, Knights of Templar and the Holy Alliance. The novelist Brown made a fortune with his *'De Vince Code'*. People love that stuff. You're getting too wrapped of in sensationalism. Forget about it. Do the job God wants you to do. If you want to bring our Church up to contemporary times, do it. Don't dwell on the past. Put those books away."

"I guess I was digressing a little," said William. "Was I ranting a little?"

"A little."

"Okay. Here's what I want. I want confession to be a general gathering. I feel people should be able to gather in the church, listen to a priest give a homily type talk – before or after Mass or any time convenient - and then the priest or bishop can absolve everyone present. If anyone wants to go to the priest on an individual basis, he or she is free to do it. I am still saying a priest or bishop still gives absolution but not in a dark closet."

"Interesting," said Peter again. "Have you heard anyone complain about the confessional?"

"Sure. Haven't you?"

"No although I guess I haven't been listening that closely."

Pope William turned away from his apartment window. "You see, Peter. I'm not picking fault with you individually. I'm picking fault with the whole Church. They don't seem to be listening. They seem to be stuck in an inflexible format. Nowhere does any rule say that this is how confession should be done. Put yourself in a sinner's shoes. Do you remember your youth? Weren't you highly intimidated by the confessional box? Once a month the nuns marched us over to the church for confession. For an hour ahead of time, I worked at thinking up some good sins that wouldn't cause Father Dubert to bawl me out. By the way, that's not his real name."

"That will not be a popular move. Most priests will not like it."

"Exactly my point. And I bet it's the elderly priests resisting. Why? Because I have read some of them – again I say just a few – get a form of sadistic joy in hearing us poor Catholics get on our knees and beg forgiveness. Jesus didn't make sinners do that. All He said was your faith has saved you. Don't you think God knows our sins? Naming our faults to a human, a man, doesn't help us improve our life. If we fail again, we are even more reluctant to go into that closet and repeat again what we confessed last month."

"William," said Cardinal Whittier, "you'll have a testy and argumentative time presenting that idea to the College of Cardinals and the Roman Curia."

"I know, but I am going to present it anyway. What do you think public opinion will be?"

"Now that I think about it, it might be quite popular. Do you sincerely think it will bring the fallen away Catholic back to the Faith?"

"It will lessen the amount of slackers. I can guarantee this, Peter. It will cease driving any away from the Church because of Reconciliation."

"If it'll help bring the people closer to God, I guess I'm all for it. If it will even bring them into the church building more often, I am definitely for it. William, keep in mind you might be bringing about a schism in the Church. You're going to have vocal and staunch resistance to any novel ideas. Look how much resistance and downright defiance our late Pope had in his reign. "

"I am aware of that," said William. "but I want to continue the streamlining and get rid of as much bureaucracy as possible. The more I read about the history of the Church, the more it aggravates me. I hated the bureaucracy of my police department back in Illinois but I was a peon. I couldn't change anything. But here, maybe I can. Maybe I can change the opinion of other denominations that we are not as rigid and inflexible as perceived. We can be tolerant of other faiths without giving up our past history."

"William, some of our hierarchy will leave the Church. Think about that. Will it be for the good or bad for the Roman Catholic faith?"

Pope William appeared thoughtful. "I don't know but for the clergy that leave the Church, I will appoint more liberal men – and possibly women – to replace them. That's what most popes did."

"William, I think..."

William interrupted Peter. "Peter. Let's step back a minute. By some unknown means, I was elected Pope. Give me your honest opinion. Do you think God performed this miracle, or phenomenon as Josip wants to call it? Do you think He actually wants me to be Pope? Do you think He wants me to interject my radical sentiments into our Church? I know there will be malicious attacks on me and probably my family."

Cardinal Whittier seemed thoughtful. "Sometimes I get extremely excited thinking of you as our leader. And sometimes I get tremendously fearful of you as Pope."

"Let me add, Peter. I don't want to infer that the sacrament of Reconciliation has driven many Catholics away from the Church. It has not. "

"I'm glad to hear that," Peter answered sounding relieved.

"So, do we move forward?" asked William.

"Let's move forward," said Peter. "The Church has weathered many other far-reaching Popes that benefited the Church. Let's hope history notes Pope William as one of them. We'll meet next week. Right now you will have to travel as much of Italy as you can for the rest of the week. You've got to start meeting the faithful here in Italy first, you and Rosalie and the boys."

"Great, next week it is. A quick question, does the Roman Curia and College of Cardinals create rules and regulations and ask the Pope to approve or does the Pope make rules and regulations and ask the Curia and Cardinals to approve? In other words, who are all these groups or synods? What do they do and what am I expected to do?"

Cardinal Whittier thought for a minute. "I doubt I can give you a quick answer. Requests for rules, regulations, clarification of the Bible or any Church teachings can come from anyone however you will have the last word. As simple as that answer may sound, believe me it is quite a bit more complicated. The best short answers I can give is; first, the Synod of Bishops. There are three; first, the current version created by Pope Paul VI is an advisory to the Pope unless the Pope endows it with deliberate power. It's called the ordinary synod. The second is the Extraordinary synod and deals with urgent matters. The third is a special synod and deals with national or regional matters.

"The College of Cardinals, meeting as a Conclave, elect the Pope, as you were elected. The origin of the Conclave is quite obscure. If they meet as a consistory, they advise the Pope. The College of Bishops decide both doctrinal and disciplinary issues. Then there's the Roman Curia also known as the villain of liberal Catholics. They reside in Rome while most bishops are home. They deal with annulments of notables, excommunications of clergy and others similar matters. There are many branches in the Curia."

"Oh," said William. "I guess I'll have to remember all that. How did the Holy See get to Rome?"

"Peter decided to locate in Rome instead of Jerusalem. The words Holy See comes from the Latin Santa Sedes meaning holy seat. You'll never remember it all. No Pope ever has." Cardinal Whittier added, "Just be prepared for Cardinal Perez and his companions in the Roman Curia to thrust a dagger in your back. I'll start working on your idea." Cardinal Whittier left the apartment shaking his head. "I guess I can expect a dagger in my back, too."

The week passed quickly and the family found the trip enjoyable albeit confusing to the Italian people. At times Pope William found his reception in the Italian countryside quite cool. They were polite at least to Rosalie and her attempt at regaining her use of the Italian language. The best reception they received was at a soccer field. David and Charles - and Pope William - kicked a soccer ball around. It brought a few cheers from the spectators. Father Thiel assured the Pope that the people will warm up to him. Rosalie was greeted most warmly in her home town even though no relatives showed up. She wasn't sure if she had any still living. Inquiries regarding her maiden name, Buchelli, brought no responses.

It was a tiring week and the Papal family was extremely grateful to return to the Vatican and their apartment Friday. They felt a little more comfortable seeing the Swiss Guards standing guard at the door to their apartment. Their maid, Lucrecia, met the couple at their door. "Mrs. - and then she stammered - I don't know what to call you."

"Just call me Rosalie, please."

"Rosalie," she timidly voiced, "I hope everything is satisfactory for you."

"I'm sure it is fine."

Father Thiel met them at the door. "Say, have you folks had dinner? I can drive you to the cafeteria if you're hungry."

Pope William said, "I'm hungry and I'm sure the boys are starved."

"Yeah, Dad. Let's go."

Father John drove the family to the cafeteria in the little cart. The priest and his four passengers were stuffed into the four passenger vehicle. They were amazed at how many tourists were still walking around the Vatican grounds.

Pope William said, "I better call Peter and tell him we're home."

"He knows," said Father John. "I told him I was taking you to dinner. He said he wants to meet with you tomorrow morning. I hate to mention this, but Cardinal Perez has been quite busy around here."

"Has he had any more meetings with his detective friend?"

"Just one that I know of. I think he's getting frustrated with the man. From what I hear from other priests, Cardinal Perez is getting more impatient and temperamental."

"I don't know if that is good or bad. For a Pope, I sure don't have a very strong faith."

Laughing, Father John said, "Don't worry, your Holiness. It's in God's hands."

CHAPTER SIXTEEN

Monday morning found Pope William in his office. Cardinals Whittier, Arrasemti, Turner, Asanti, Reardon, Balino, Raymundo, Cesario, McMillan, Flanis, Marshall and Madelo gathered around in any chairs available. Cardinal Whittier also invited several bishops that he knew would be receptive to new and daring ideas. Some were members of the congregation of the Roman Curia. Most were ill at ease knowing full well what this meeting was about.

Still feeling uncomfortable in his position as Pope, William asked Cardinal Whittier to open the meeting with a prayer.

After doing so, Pope William said, "Gentlemen, I still don't know why I am here but I am, for the time being, going to assume God desires me to be your leader. I have tried to think what it is in me that God wants me to express. I have been a practicing Catholic all my life, at least since the age of reason. As of late several things in our faith have bothered me. I will enumerate little by little. Cardinal Whittier has heard me expound on them. I know he has cringed at the thought of me presenting these beliefs to you, and to the Church as a whole.

"While in Illinois as a simple policeman, the leadership of the previous Pope got me thinking. Wow, this Pope really wants to modernize the Catholic Faith. I liked his ideas. Before he had a chance to develop them God called him to his reward. Somehow I am the Pope. I want to carry on. I hope that is what the Holy Spirit desires of me.

"I want your opinion on the Sacrament of Reconciliation. As a child I, and the rest of my classmates, called it going to the closet. I want to make going into the closet an option. I want to have the act of Reconciliation to be an open assembly. The faithful can gather in the Church before or after Mass or whenever the bishop and pastor decide. They can listen to a short homily given by the priest. He can discuss the sin of the month if you will. Then he can give absolution to the group. If a person wants an individual meeting with the priest, he or she can do that. The reason for this change is I feel confessing your sins in a closet can be intimidating. I know it is what keeps some Catholics away from the Church. Once a person gives up on one of the Church's precepts, they begin to abandon other requirements or obligations of the faith. For example, if a soccer team is getting unmercifully trounced, the losing team gives up the spirit. I know from experience how that happens to fallen away Catholics.

"Many parents in my parish in Illinois have complained to me about their children abandoning Catholicism in their twenties and turning to other denominations. They felt their reconciliation of sin was between them and God. As I have told Cardinal Whittier some of our flock has been turned off to the faith by a priest taking an obvious delight in having the sinner repeat their sins over and over. Some priests make the sinner go into great detail about their sin, especially sins of purity, and most especially women. There is no need for that. God knows our sins. I would like each of you to think and pray about this. I would like to issue an edict in the next week or two about this change. I know some here are Canon Lawyers. I would like your thoughtful input. Contact as many of your bishops and priests as you can. Talk to other Cardinals. Cardinal Whittier and I want to issue an edict declaring the change soon. One requirement still remains. A priest or bishop must still be the one administrating absolution.

"I might add too that our requirement to always attend Sunday Mass isn't a major impediment to Catholics. Look how crowded other denomination's parking lots are – and it isn't a requirement of their church. Most people feel a need to pray to their creator. I feel no need to change the third commandment. I would never dare to eliminate or change any of God's commandments.

"The next item I would like to address is annulment. The Church does not explain it very well. The average population and even Catholics think it is just our form of divorce. It's just a way to make money. Well, it isn't. What we should explain more succinctly is that the requirements of a true marriage must be the presence in spirit and reality is a man, a woman and God. If any one of the three is missing, it's not a valid marriage. For example, it the man does not intend to be faithful or the woman does not intend to have children, it's grounds for an annulment. There never was a marriage. If God was not present, for example a couple saying they were married on a deserted island without a priest, it's not a valid marriage. That's what an annulment declares. An annulment just states one of the three requirements was missing. And the cost is simply a paperwork fee. It's not thousands of dollars as rumored.

"I also feel the Church deals quite harshly with divorced Catholics. We don't let them participate in any of our services. We should understand there will always be a situation when two people cannot live together for whatever reason. They will have to receive an annulment by the Church and receive a divorce as required by civil laws. We shouldn't shun them and force them to live outside the Church. If they accept the fact that an annulment is needed to remarry, they should be allowed to receive the Sacraments.

"The last item is our alleged praying to the saints. Other denominations fault us for that practice. I don't believe we actually pray to the saints. We ask them to intercede for us to God. I would compare it to having a friend in city hall. If we had a problem with our street, we would ask that friend to intercede for us. Since the saints are standing right next to God, who else to ask for help?

"Thank you for listening to me. Be honest. If you think I am way out of line, tell me. Peter has told me of some of the injurious consequences of changes or clarifications like this can bring about. I can assure you, God willing, there will only be a few more simplifications."

With that, the group closed with a prayer and left the room. Pope William felt it odd no one had any questions, arguments or comments as they left. Pope William found himself sweating profusely. Cardinal Whittier remained.

"Well Peter," said William, "What do you think?"

"Cardinal Turner said to me as he left that he liked the thought about Reconciliation. He has never liked the confessional and agreed with your annulment discussion."

"That's possibly one man on our side."

"One of the many we will need," said Cardinal Whittier. "William, the way this will have to go is we will need many Cardinals, bishops, priests and even laity on our side. We will need to send out a trial edict to all the Cardinals and bishops in all countries. Then we will study their responses. From that we'll make a decision. Most likely we will have to make some modifications to our edict. Some of our clergy are already on the fringe of leaving the Church, primarily on the role of woman. Some want to start their own denomination. They want to act as Martin Luther did. He didn't like the Pope giving orders although his main objection was the selling of indulgences as Pope Leo X did to raise money to build Saint Peter's Basilica. The same defection could happen now."

The young new Pope said, "Luther also said the Pope can't reinterpret scripture. Do you believe that?"

"You've done a lot of reading in your short tenure as Pope, haven't you?"

"Yes I have. I was surprised his friends had to hide him after the 1521 Edict of Worms was published. He was noted as a convicted heretic subject to persecution and possibly death. Didn't he also say 'Faith alone will save you'?"

Cardinal Whittier said, "Yes he did say that. I believe a pope can make his own interpretation of scripture or as you say put his spin on it. That is why there is a plethora of advisors at a pope's call. The Cardinals can get quite animated discussing a Pope's many publishings but they seem to always be more reserved in debating viewpoints in the Pope's presence."

Pope William said, "I do believe from what I've read though, a Pope can reinterpret what a previous Pope has interpreted. They are only human, too."

Cardinal Whittier nodded. "I must say you sure interpret a lot of what you interpret."

The young Pope smiled. "Peter, do you think I have taken on an insurmountable task? Have I bitten off more than I can chew? After reading and seeing firsthand the politics involved, maybe the momentum of the Church's direction can't be changed. I suddenly feel like St. Peter. I can't walk on water. Maybe I should resign and go back to Peoria and be a dumb cop."

"William, let's not throw in the towel yet. Let's see what kind of responses we get. Then we will see if God is behind us or has abandoned us."

"I think I will go into the chapel and pray," said William. "You know? The only time I prayed before all this was when I had to pull over a speeding auto at night. Approaching a car with blackened windows was quite intimidating." Pope William stood straighter. "Let us not mess around with a trial edict. If no Cardinal or bishop has any major conflicts with what I've said, let's publish the edict. I don't feel I have a lot of time."

"Saints preserve us," said the Cardinal. "I can understand. Yes, William. Let's publish and pray. Go pray and I will too."

To the venerable Cardinals, Archbishops, Bishops, Priests, Brothers and Sisters. Humbly accepting that God has directed me to be your representative of Christ, I send this edict out to all of our faithful. A private confession to a clergyman is nowhere mandated in the Holy Bible. It allegedly began in Ireland around the eighteenth or nineteenth century. It seems some of the Irish clergy wanted to know the secret sins of the royalty. Looking at the practice objectively, it is easy to see how it can lead to abuses. The abuses were cast mainly by a minority of our priests upon women and children. At this point in our history of alleged clergy abuses, we need to no longer place our vulnerable children in harm's way. A one on one meeting with a priest and a child is not recommended and is making temptation entirely too convenient for those whose faith is fragile. While such problems are rare, one occurrence is one too many.

A suitable method of Reconciliation will now be a general confession by a priest or bishop. Following the confession, a general absolution will be given. A gathering before or after Mass or any time suitable to the confessor and penitents can be arranged by the bishop of each parish in conjunction with the parish priest. A private meeting can still be observed if so desired by the penitent. Jesus forgave sinners on the spot.

This procedure shall begin immediately.

Pope William.

CHAPTER SEVENTEEN

After waiting several days, comments began to flow in to the layman Pope, Pope William. Cardinal Whittier fielded the responses and prepared to read them to William.

"So, William," said Peter, "I have some of the early results. What do you think they will be?"

"Oh, don't play with me, Peter. Give it to me straight."

"Here's one of them. A young priest in Ohio said, 'Great. I've hated confession since I was a child', and an older priest from Arkansas says, 'I have always disliked having more priests in for Christmas or Easter confessions than parishioners'."

"What's the bottom line?"

"Wait. Here's a good one. A priest in Toronto said, 'Anything that gets people in the church building more often is good.' A priest and bishop from here in Italy said, 'Divorce has driven many Catholics from the Church'. He feels Reconciliation the problem. Many Catholics have thrown out the baby with the bathwater."

Nervously pacing the room, Pope William said, "Okay, okay, what's the results? What's the percentage?"

"So far about 70 to 30 in favor. Not many results in from South America or the Far East yet."

"Peter, how many times have I said I feel like St. Peter walking on water? I shouldn't be here. I should be driving my police cruiser around Peoria."

"You've said it a lot – too many times actually."

Pope William said, "Okay. This is only Tuesday. Let's see what we have by Friday."

"William, I do have some encouraging news, though. We are starting to get requests from several countries for you to visit them. Especially the United States."

"Really?"

"Yes," said Peter. "You're quite a novelty."

"I hope you mean that in a good way. I don't want to be something of a freak show. I want people to see me as someone who will improve the Church. I want to be seen as someone who sincerely wants to mend some of our faults. I want us to be more acceptable to our congregation. I want us to appear as warm and welcome as Jesus was to saints and sinners alike. I don't think we've been that way lately. Peter, I want to impress our people that God had chosen me to do this thing without appearing arrogant or pretentious. Oh my God! Please help me to appear holy."

"You know, William?" said Peter. "I think recently you have been sounding more like a pope than a policeman. You might get the hang of this pope business yet."

The Pope sank in his plush recliner he had shipped here from Illinois. "Rosalie said my hair is suddenly getting grayer. I think I see why so many popes appear stooped shouldered."

"Yes, there is a lot of weight on your shoulders. William, I am taking the liberty to schedule you for a few visits to some countries. I think you should visit Germany, Brazil and even Cuba now that we've opened communications with them. Then we'll shoot for the Far East."

"No, I can't yet."

"Yes you can and you will."

"You want me out of Dodge before the shooting starts."

Peter laughed. "I guess you could say that. But actually, it will be good for you to get out and mix with the faithful – and the not so faithful."

"I'd like to visit the United States first."

"No. I think it's best to start in Europe and South America first. We don't want to show favoritism."

"Okay. Question," said William. "Since you're going to be assigned here, who should I name to replace you?"

"That's easy. Bishop John W. Hobbs. He's a bishop in Chicago."

"Isn't the public going to accuse us of favoritism?"

Peter said, "Probably, but that's okay."

"Okay, show me how to do that. Then let's meet Friday and see where we stand in public opinion."

"Don't forget, tomorrow at ten we are meeting with a group of nuns from England."

"I'll be there."

Peter smiled and left the room.

The meeting with the nuns from England went well for Pope William. The nuns, however, were very much concerned about the role of women in the Church. William could see some aggravation and impatience with the slow advances for their gender. The new Pope could appreciate and agree with their plight. He told the women he would try honestly to make encroachments in the Church's men-only attitude. He made sure Cardinal Whittier was present as well as Cardinals Antonio Larenzo and Mario Fantelli, each a Canon lawyer. The Pope was quick to notice glances from the lawyers to Cardinal Whittier, who quickly looked away. Due to clever maneuvering William was able to say nothing that would be considered blasphemous or downright outrageous. Mentally, however, Pope William coined a new phrase. "The stained glass ceiling". He intended to break it. He determined to try out the phrase later with Cardinal Whittier.

After the nuns left, the two lawyers remained seated. Cardinal Whittier said, "Well, William. I can see you are laying some groundwork for future obstacles."

One of the canon lawyers, Cardinal Larenzo, said, "Your holiness, certainly you realize that you are setting yourself up for Josip to sabotage any attempt to change the role of women in the Catholic Church. I won't say whether we agree with you or not but he has set as his mission an undertaking to force you to resign. Do not make it too easy for him."

"I'm aware of that, Antonio, but Peter and I have decided to accept my being elected as a miracle. If so, then I must do what I feel should be done. If it turns out that I am here by some hoax, then I will quickly resign and it will be up to you Cardinals and the Roman Curia to accept or redo all that I have accomplished."

"Accomplished," said Cardinal Larenzo. "That's a righteous word to use. You must feel you are doing God's work. Do you?"

"Antonio, I have to. If I do not feel I am doing the right thing, then I should pack up my family and return to the United States and be a cop. I will state flatly that unless Josip finds fraud, I will not resign."

"Then use caution and proceed slowly." With that the two lawyers rose to leave the room. "Oh, what's the result of your confession edict?"

"Peter," said William, "tell them."

"We're running almost eighty percent approvals."

"Really? That's amazing."

"Yes it is," said Peter.

Cardinal Larenzo said, "Don't forget about all the other little problems we have."

"I know. Peter and I have been considering our chain of command. I feel we are top heavy and possess too much dead weight. That is the reason there is so much bureaucracy, and I might add, corruption. I asked Peter to pick some Canon Lawyers that were vibrant and open minded to be here today. That's why you and Mario are present.

Cardinal Larenzo laughed, "I guess that means our jobs are safe?"

"Yes, definitely. The Japanese have a saying – and I paraphrase – when the business is faltering, remove personnel from the top, not the workers – or should I say achievers - at the bottom."

"I can almost say," said Cardinal Fantelli, "I hope Josip's detective doesn't find any deceit in your election."

"I agree," said Cardinal Larenzo. "I can't wait for the next chapter."

After the two Canon Lawyers left the room, Peter said, "William, give me a heads up. What things in our Church are you planning for future turmoil? I feel you have already decided on an agenda. Am I correct?"

"Peter you are right. There are so many minor problems in our Church to be dealt with. Day to day little troubles that are almost as important as big obstacles are arriving on my desk constantly. I read the communications reaching me every day and I don't know what to do. Of course I first have to get them translated. I realize this is an extremely volatile place. There is a bishop on the east coast of the United States expounding about birth control. A priest in South America has his own interpretation regarding whether Christ was married to Mary Magdalen. A theologian in Europe is insisting Christ had brothers and sisters. The bishop there wants me to excommunicate him."

"William, that's only the beginning. But I'll say one thing, though. I've read those letters and they, and many others, are looking to you as their redeemer on Earth."

"Oh my God. Oops. I guess I shouldn't say that."

"Oh my gosh would be more appropriate."

"I am fifty-one. Josip said that's young as popes go. I could be at this job for a long time. I don't know if I can take it for twenty, thirty or forty more years."

The Cardinal looked ever more studious. "That's why God doesn't let us see the future. We couldn't take it."

"I agree."

"Again, what's on your immediate agenda?" asked Peter.

"I hesitate to say, but here goes. Priest's celibacy. It's ridiculous. Another is birth control. The Church is against it because it wastes the sperm. Doesn't the rhythm method have the same result? The Bible interpreters jumped on God ending the life of Onan because he wasted his seed. It wasn't the wasting of seed that God hated, it was he denied his late brother's wife of an heir. And bringing a child into the world when he can't be properly fed or cared for is immoral. I am also against the death penalty. We don't explain ourselves very well to the public. Why don't we take the time and care to explain our tenets. Consider annulment. So many non-Catholics think it is just our word for divorce. Why are we so stand-offish? Other Baptized members of different faiths are not allowed to receive Communion? Priests once told me, as a Eucharistic minister, do not judge people coming up to receive the Body of Christ. God is big enough to take care of Himself."

"All right, William," said Peter. "Give me the big one."

"Women. Why do a few of these old Cardinals seem to foster misogyny – the hatred of women? Why do some feel women are not equal to men? They appear to wish a woman to only do household chores. Doesn't the Catholic Church realize a woman is the only way a new life comes into our world? At the moment of conception God has to be present to create a soul. He is standing right next to the woman. At the time of conception the man could be a thousand miles away. A woman's body is a miracle machine. All we men can do better is lifting a heavier box. The Catholic Church treats a woman as they do in the Arab and Muslim countries. And finally, why is a virgin so much better than a mother? Look at the pain of childbirth. For nine months a woman goes through nausea and discomfort just to bring new life into the world. I doubt we men could stand it.

"I could talk on the stupidity of virginity for hours. Why is virginity so wonderful and holy? Why do our Church Scholars talk incessantly about a virgin being spotless? Why does having intercourse – which I might add was created by God – put a spot on a woman? Why doesn't a spot appear on a man? Have you holy men ever thought about this Bible verse? In Genesis 1:28 God blessed them, (Adam and Eve) saying: 'Be fertile and multiply; fill the earth and subdue it'. Could a virgin not be fulfilling God's will by maintaining virginity? Maybe she's committing a sin? I know. I'm being facetious, but think of that.

"How about this? What if every woman on Earth remained a virgin? They'd all go straight to heaven, right? Do I have to answer that ridiculous question? Read P. D. James's book *Children of Men*. After one generation there would be no humans left on Earth. A question came up in my bible class. Did God make a mistake? How was Adam supposed to multiply if he was the only human God created?

"While we're on the subject, why is the sex act so foul? Why is the pleasure of the sex act so disgusting? God created the act of intercourse. He created the feeling of pleasure. Intercourse in marriage is good and should be enjoyed. Look how the Church's idea of the sex act has amended over the centuries. There was a time in the early Church when a married couple was forbidden to receive Holy Communion after intercourse until they went to Confession. How ridiculous. There is so much wrong in our interpretation of sex it is unbelievable how much it has been misconstrued and made to seem repulsive. And who made sex so bad and vile? God didn't do it; man did, with Satan's encouragement. You know what else is so strange to me?" asked Pope William. "Why can television show all kinds of killings, cruel tortures, bloody butchering and dismembering of a human but the sex act – which was created by God – cannot be shown? I know. You don't have to tell me. I'm not fostering sex on television. It is odd how the act of intercourse has been distorted into something vile and naughty."

Cardinal Whittier as so often occurred after one of the Pope's rhetorical question remained silent.

"I'm reminded of a question asked of me at the Peoria Airport, 'When can you and Rosalie have sex?' Why was that question asked? It's never been asked of the president and the first lady. You see? The sex act seems to have a special place in society. It should be as normal as eating a pizza. Murder wasn't created by God."

"William, are you going to advocate the ordination of women?"

Pope William began pacing the floor. "Peter, I can't honestly answer that. I want to discuss it with our Canon Lawyers and any Cardinal or bishop that will listen to me with an open mind."

"May God help you and may God help us," was all that Cardinal Whittier could say.

"I need to go to my chapel and pray some more," said Pope William.

"Me too," said Cardinal Peter. "Tell Rosalie hello for me. Also, let me advise you of a tact other Popes have taken. You seem to have a delicate and definitely challenging agenda ahead of you. What they have done, and you should bear this in mind, they appointed bishops and Cardinals who think as they did. Yes, William. It is politics as usual."

"You'll have to advise me."

"I know. Oh, one other thing. One of your sons almost beheaded Cardinal Perez with a soccer ball."

"Ah!"

CHAPTER EIGHTEEN

"Do you see this? Do you see this?" Cardinal Perez screamed at Cardinals Paulo and Peligrini. "Barely three months as Pope and he's making changes in confession. He's making wholesale changes in our sacred sacrament of Reconciliation. I will not let this happen! He's ..."

Cardinal Peligrini interrupted, "Josip. Take it easy. You're going to have a heart attack."

"William is going to have a heart attack if I have any choice in the matter. God damn him!"

"Josip, lately your manner of speech isn't becoming of a Cardinal," said Cardinal Paulo.

"You're going to hear a lot worse language if we don't stop this man. This Satan!" Josip was walking around his office, wildly waving his arms. "Gentlemen, I am waiting for a sign from God. I feel He will give me a sign on how to stop him. Sometimes we in the Church, we in control, must do something drastic. I feel it is coming to that. God wants me to stop this heathen."

The Cardinals looked at each other. "Josip, you're bordering on insanity. This could quite possibly be a miracle."

"Don't give me that ..." Josip paused. "Listen to me. I've done a poll. I have fifteen Cardinals who'll back any move I make. I don't know where you two stand but they want me to take action. Gentlemen, I can guarantee I will, and soon, before any other desecrations occur."

Cardinal Peligrini said, "Josip, I'd advise caution. I have received word that a few of my bishops support this change in Reconciliation. Even their priests have lauded it. And all my bishops haven't contacted me yet. This may be a good move."

"Vincent, what is the matter with you? Can't you see what's happening? Can't you see what he is doing?" Continuing his screaming and cursing, Josip added, "I tell you this. He's a married man and he will be trying to have women ordained. I WILL NOT LET IT HAPPEN! If I have to remove him myself, I will do it! It's God's will!"

"What are you implying, Josip?" asked Cardinal Paulo.

"I am not implying a damn thing. I am swearing before God I will personally remove him any way possible."

"If this is a miracle, Josip, then you are putting yourself in danger of serious sin. What do you mean by personally remove him?"

"Understand it any way you want. God will see to his death. Take it any way you want. I may have to be God's finger on Earth."

Cardinals Peligrini and Paulo stood up. "Josip, we're leaving. I think you should see your confessor."

As the two Cardinals left Josip's office, they closed the door behind them. Cardinal Paulo said, "Vincent, I am wondering if we should see His Holiness, Pope William. I think maybe Josip should be removed from his status of Cardinal-Camerlengo; Maybe even reduced to bishop or priest. "

"I think I agree," said Cardinal Peligrini. "I've never seen Josip so violent. Do you think he would do harm to Pope William?"

"It's allegedly been accomplished centuries ago. I have some reservations about the Pope too, but I also wonder if this is a miracle. I wanted to add that I have had a favorable response from quite a few of my bishops and priests regarding confession."

"I know. Many other Cardinals have told me their reactions have been absolutely favorable. Some have told me they have seen parishioners in the Church edifice they haven't seen in years."

Cardinal Paulo said, "Let's go talk to Peter. By now he should have results from at least eighty or ninety other Cardinals."

"This is taking a lot of time," said Cardinal Peligrini. "I expected to be back in my diocese by now."

CHAPTER NINETEEN

Cardinal Whittier walked into Pope William's office. Rosalie was dusting the pope's desk lamp. "Aren't the housekeeping maids doing a good enough job?" he said.

"Yes. I just need to be doing something," she said. "I have so little to do."

"Sister Rachel says you seem to have a true talent for painting. She showed me some of your paintings. You Italians all seem to have artistic blood. I can't paint a board."

"Every time I go into the Museum, I feel so inadequate. I can spend hours in there. William, did you know in the museum there is a circular staircase called the Bramante Staircase in a double helix that allows people going up to not see people going down? Pope Julius II started the museum as a display for sculptures but Popes Clement XIV and Pius VI also made it a museum of art."

"That's why it's there. It's for all to enjoy." The Cardinal looked over at Pope William sitting at his desk and said to Rosalie, "Could you get William down to work? Maybe you can get him to look at all these communiques and letters. I know he has a few far-reaching contemplations in his head."

"I was worried about the ceremonies," said William. "I think All Saints Day and All Souls Day went off without a hitch. It sure seemed odd for the Pope to not be the one to say Mass. I hope Christmas goes just as well."

"It will," said Peter, "but in the meantime you have to answer those correspondences on your desk."

Pope William frowned at Peter. "I know. I have my 'far-reaching contemplations' sorted out. Actually I have been waiting for you to help me. How do I present them to the College of Cardinals and Roman Curia?"

"I'll arrange it after we return from our trip. I think you should make a statement about the killings in Africa. Almost fifty children were killed."

"I know. Help me write something."

"Then there is that big civil strike up North. There's been some injuries."

"Peter, why does God allow people to hurt themselves and others?"

"Because God gave mankind free will. Here's your itinerary."

"Thanks. I have been waiting for you to give it to me. I think I have ten nations waiting to see me. When will I have time to answer those letters and requests for solutions to our people's problems?"

"You'll have to do that while we're flying around the world. I've arranged to have several Canon Lawyers and several other bishops to go with us. We'll work on those problems. Are you prepared to go with us, Rosalie?"

"I suppose so," she said as she shook her dust cloth out the window. "Oh my goodness!" she said. "People are waving at me!"

"Rosalie my dear," said the Cardinal. "You've become almost as popular as your husband. All the nuns in the world are clamoring to have you visit them, especially the younger nuns. It's like the first lady in the states. They want to know how much influence you have with your husband."

"Very little," said Rosalie. "Can the boys go too?"

"Definitely," said the Cardinal.

William said, "You influence me plenty. Actually it was your tacit approval that led me to this job."

"I'm not too sure," she said.

Cardinal Whittier sat in a very uncomfortable chair in front of the new pope's desk. "I think one of your important tasks is to get some softer chairs. Besides that, have you looked at these correspondences?"

"Yes. I can't believe how many dilemmas are going on in church. There is a pedophile complaint in New York, City, a woman in South Africa claims she is carrying a priest's child, an alcoholic priest in Mexico City, a laity member in Tokyo claiming a teaching nun is a lesbian, a Los Angeles deacon accusing his parish priest of stealing from the Sunday collection basket. A priest in Canada wants to use Latin when saying Mass. The laity want French. Does God care what language we use? It goes on and on. What do I do? Are we that bad?"

Cardinal Whittier took on a somber mood, "William, let's put things in perspective. The Catholic Church isn't alone in their internal problems. It just seems the press gives us the most coverage. As I have said before, since we are perceived as the most stand-offish and uppity of religious denominations – and we probably are - the press just can't seem to wait until one of our clergy do something offensive and provoking. They seem to rush to post it on the evening news. Other denominations have their problems, too."

"I do not recall anything lately on the late night news programs about another denomination's pedophile problem. Like I told you earlier, when we arrived at the Peoria Airport, a reporter just couldn't wait to ask me about sex. When can Rosalie and I have sex? It as though we're not supposed to have relations even though we're married."

Cardinal Whittier said, "It's not that, William. It's that they haven't had an occasion to ask a religious that kind of question. You'll have to face a fact. No matter what, you're a novelty. You can't blame them. I guess we can blame that on Satan. Probably it will never change."

"I suppose so," said William.

"Now William, let's look at these appalling situations before you. A good leader knows how to delegate each incident to those most proficient in handling them. I can recommend Cardinals for each type of problem. You can allocate certain predicaments to the ones I feel can process them most adroitly. Then, you will have them bring their solutions back to you for your approval or disapproval."

"I guess that makes sense," said William.

"The tough one is going to be that bishop who wants to ordain a nun. He seems to have quite a following, especially women. William, I hope you realize there may be a time when you'll have to excommunicate someone."

William swiveled around in his seat. "I feel about that as I did when I had to carry a pistol as a policeman; I never had to use it."

"Just keep it in mind," said Peter. "That's a good analogy; a weapon."

"That woman thing is sure a thorn in the Catholic Church. Could you set up a meeting with some Canon Lawyers for me? I want to discuss woman's role in the Church and also some Bible teachings."

"Oh William, William. Speaking of guns, you sure don't evade any bullets directed at you. Cardinal Perez is champing at the bit to attack you. I'll say one thing, though. You seem to be gathering a sizeable following. There are times I feel God has surely performed a miracle by having you elected pope. Then there are times I just scratch my head."

"Peter, I want to do an experiment."

"Tell me about it on our flight to Chicago. You have to name Bishop John Hobbs to be elected to Cardinal in Chicago. The diocese wants to make it a big occasion, and rightly so. We also have four elderly Cardinals retiring. You will have to name replacements for them."

Rosalie stopped her dusting. "You know? The more I hear the going ons between you two, the more I feel the Church is operating just like a big business."

"It is, Rosalie. It is a big unwieldy business. William, let's look at our itinerary again."

Father Francis, Pope William's secretary, walked in the Pope's office. "Your Holiness, Cardinals Peligrini and Paulo would like a minute with you."

"Sure, send them in."

The two Cardinals entered somewhat reservedly. "Your Holiness," said Cardinal Peligrini. "Hello Mrs. Meier, Hello Peter. We'd like to have a word with you, your Holiness. We're not sure how to begin."

"Sit down. And please call me William." Cardinal Whittier and Rosalie remained in the office.

"William," said Vincent, "I am not sure Mrs. Meier should hear what we have to say."

"It's okay. I try to keep her informed," said William.

"As you probably know, we haven't been too receptive of your appointment. Maybe we're too old to accept the happenings that have occurred lately, but we're trying."

William said, "I understand completely. I can tell you honestly I still get moments of tremendous doubt when realizing where I am and what I am doing. If I were still a policeman in Illinois, I would be feeling just as you. What can I do for you?"

"It's Cardinal Perez. I don't want to feel like a tattle-tale child in grade school but I...we feel he is most angry. We feel he is letting your appointment affect his mental well-being. To be sure, we were and are still unbelieving. We still feel your election was a hoax or fraud but definitely not perpetrated by you. We most assuredly feel you are a good and Christian man. But, William, Josip just might do something drastic. I hate to say this but he told us he feels he is the finger of God. Your Holiness, he wants you to die."

Cardinal Whittier and Rosalie gasped in unison. "Vincent, did he say that?" said Peter.

"Yes."

Pope William smiled, "Gentlemen, as a former policeman it is not the first time someone has wanted me to die but do you feel he might do something to hasten my death?"

"William, we don't exactly know the extent of his hatred for you but with his emotions growing more out of hand each day, well... we just don't know. We thought it prudent to let you know."

Cardinal Whittier spoke, "Do you think we should inform the Swiss Guards?"

Cardinal Paulo shook his head. "I really don't know. Quite possibly we're being alarmists."

William teasingly said, "Should I get a royal taster?"

"William," said Rosalie. "Don't make light of this."

"I don't mean to, my dear. Fredrico, how angry did he seem?"

"Very," said the Cardinal. "I guess I should say his language was most unbecoming of a Cardinal."

"What do you recommend, Peter?"

"Let's go to the source. Let's talk to him and sound him out. We'll see if we can get a feeling how dangerous he could be. If it appears he could be threatening, I'll alert the Swiss Guards and do some checking on the kitchen personnel."

"William," said Rosalie, "I never thought there would be this type of problem in the Vatican. I don't like it."

"Rosalie, have you forgotten your life back in Illinois? As a policeman I was in danger every day."

Rosalie sat back down. "I was just getting to enjoy life here. Now this."

"I'm sorry to have to bring this kind of news to you, your Holiness."

"Don't worry. I am glad you did. There is no life perfectly safe. Most rich and famous people have armed guards. There have been several attempts to do harm at different popes. We will talk to Josip."

"Josip knows we were quite unhappy with the direction of his dialogue. We don't mind if you tell him we were the ones bringing you the information."

"Thank you, very much," said William.

Peter said, "I guess I am not too surprised. I will spread this information to the proper channels."

William turned to Rosalie, "Rosalie, I want you to think about this. My job as a policeman was much more dangerous than this. I don't think Josip will go around carrying a gun or knife. I feel we can settle him down. I will give him a meaningful post and try to make him feel more worthwhile. I will make him a part of discussions we have regarding changes in the Church. I have found every person on Earth has something to contribute. We just have to seek it out."

"I hope so, Bill, I mean William," said Rosalie.

"You know, Rosalie," said Cardinal Whittier, "William just might be a good choice as Pope yet."

"Peter," said the Pope. "I definitely do not want to travel around in that auto with the bullet proof glass you guys have made up for Popes."

"The Pope Mobile? It shouldn't be needed. We're traveling in some fairly friendly countries. However, you have had some death threats you know."

"I know, but I will not use the auto."

Rosalie said, "I surely thought the Pope would have less death threats than the president."

"Considering how William was elected you can see how your husband would cause some unbalanced individual to want him dead."

"Yeah," said William. "We have a Cardinal right under our noses not happy with the situation."

"I don't want to even think about it," said Rosalie.

"William," said Peter. "Don't be stubborn. Think of your Swiss Guards and the men sworn to protect you. Do you want to make it extra hard on them? They took it quite seriously when John Paul II was attacked."

"I'll think about it."

CHAPTER TWENTY

The Christmas services at Vatican City became quite an event. Pope William handled the occasion fairly well with Cardinal Whittier and Cardinal Perez concelebrating Mass. Cardinal Perez seemed content performing all blessing occasions. Catholics around the world were wondering how the Pope would appear before the world. Pope William and his family participated in most of the Christmas events and attended all occasions of Christmas pageantry. They even sang some carols. Charles and David agreed they were as good as the von Trapp family. Charles joshed that we should call ourselves the von Meier family chorale ensemble.

The Pope had just finished Epiphany services when he called Cardinal Whittier and several other Cardinals into his office.

"Okay William," Cardinal Whittier said. "What is it?"

"It's time to discuss celibacy, "William said. "I am going to send out a trial balloon to the College of Cardinals and Roman Curia."

"William, do you really think it needs to be discussed? Our Church has flourished for centuries as is. Why mess with it?"

"Peter. You know why. The Church hasn't flourished. Wait. That's incorrect. The Church has flourished. Do you know why? The early Church leaders made changes. They updated. They made Church teachings more contemporary. It had to, to survive. Some changes were noble and popular. Some were not. I feel the time has come to make adjustments. I feel I have some good visions – just a few.

"And here's why. Look how many priests and nuns are revoking their vows of obedience, poverty and chastity. Then they even leave the Church. Look at the problem we're having getting young men and women to enter the clergy. Have you seen the status of our missionary churches at home and abroad? Many priests have to cover three and four parishes and in some places the parishioners don't even have regular Sunday Mass. Why are we so stubborn about celibacy? Our first Pope was married with children. There have been several others since then. Other denominations have survived with married clergy, why not us? The church survived its first three centuries without practicing celibacy. Why suddenly pretend it's a directive from God or it's always been demanded in the Bible? "

"It's in the Bible, William." Cardinal Redaro Icarcion said. "St. Paul said it in 1 Corinthians 8 vs. 32:34, a married man has to see to the needs of his spouse, a married woman has to see to the needs of her spouse."

"The Bible. That's another problem. Where does that translation say a man or woman must be celibate in order to properly perform as a member of the clergy? It says he or she must attend to his or her needs but it does not assert they must be celibate. Granted a married clergyman or clergywoman may have more distractions but can you honestly say they will not serve suitably? Have you heard of spin? A news anchorman puts his spin on an article. Are we so sure that Corinthians section was interpreted properly? Does it mean a priest can be married or not? I think Church scholars use Bible scripture John3:29 – it's the only place in the Bible using the word 'bride' - and Ephesians 5:24 that states 'as the church is subordinate to Christ, so wives be subordinate to their husbands in everything' as a metaphor or symbol that we must be faithful to Christ. I don't think we can truthfully say it means all clergy must be celibate.

"And translation. The word of God was first handed down by word of mouth. Then the Bible was written in Greek. It was then translated into Latin – various forms of Latin I might add. Peter and Paul didn't speak Latin, they spoke the koine Greek of all Jewish Diaspora. Next, a fourth century bishop Damasus, the bishop of Rome, asked some guy named Jerome to translate the Bible into a standard form of Latin. He had so much trouble translating it he even contradicted himself. He even admitted picking out what he thought was the best interpretation and then he went back and made changes again. In the next two centuries many unnamed editors made translations and were dispensed until finally the Vulgate version was declared official. Even the

Vulgate omits sections and psalms. The basic inspirations may have come from God but humans, being human, didn't always get it right.

"Gentlemen, look at it this way. Back at St. Sabina I led a Bible discussion group. Before I began reading this material about the early Church, and the early versions of the Bible, I believed the Bible I had in my hands was unchanged down through the ages. I believed what Moses and the other Old Testament writers wrote – and what the New Testament writers wrote – was the original and untouched words handed down by God. Just like the Ten Commandments, written in stone. But you know Bible verses were not written in stone. You knowledgeable men know of the many changed, rewritten and reinterpreted Bibles we now have. Our Bible is full of footnotes, telling us what each verse means. I think there are more footnotes than Bible verses. If God inspired the writers exactly like He wanted, why are there so many changes? Did God suddenly realize He made a mistake? Did God say, 'Oops! My Gospel writer didn't get it right? I better re-inspire the writer more clearly what I meant.' Now you know that didn't happen. The human element caused the need to rewrite and reinterpret the Bible.

"And, in comparison, the Ten Commandments were written in stone. Have any of the Church Fathers made any changes in the Commandments? No. There have been no changes since there was no need for interpretations. The words were in stone. No need for someone to reinterpret what was written.

"Also, speaking of Bible interpretation, do you really think Adam went around with eleven ribs on one side and twelve on the other side?"

"William, William, "Peter said. "What are you doing? Are you planning to revamp 2000 years of the Church? Are you going to redo the Bible too?"

"No Peter," said William, "I just want to make it reasonably palpable. I want to add common sense to our Catholic Church. There are so many things in our teachings that leave a vacuum. And when you have a vacuum, people fill it in with rumors, myths and just plain lies. And what do we do? We look the other way and say, 'That's just the way it is'."

"William, you can't correct centuries of conceivable errors or misconceptions in just a few years."

"I know but I want to start. I believe in God. A lot of people do. I believe in Jesus Christ. I believe in the Mother of God's virgin birth. I believe the bread and wine at Consecration is truly the body and blood of Jesus. God can do whatever He wants. What I want to know is how can mere mortal men – and men only – write an unbiased account of the Word of God? Why weren't any of the Bible writers women? Do you know why? They were not allowed to be educated. They were never taught to write. What if the first human God created was a woman?"

"William! Don't start that. The Gospel writers were inspired."

"Yes, the thought was inspired by God but the human handing down by word of mouth and then putting it down on paper quite possibly didn't get it exactly right. Every Catholic scholar teaching the Bible admits there are a lot of vacant spaces in the first two centuries of Church History where guesses and assumptions were written. Somehow they morphed into infallible facts. Disagreeing became an excommunicating event. That's why I believe the New Testament is more accurate than the Old Testament. It seems to be more verbatim.

"Look at the United State history. We had people who could read and write and still they didn't consistently get American History right. Peter, you're a learned man. Tell me I have it wrong."

Cardinal Whittier remained silent.

"Gentlemen," said William. "As a child I often played a game called 'telephone'. Fifteen or twenty children sat in a circle. The first person whispered a sentence to the second person. That person in turn whispered it to the third person and so on until it circled the group. As you can expect, at the end the sentence was nowhere near the same."

The Cardinals were restless but did listen intently.

"Now do you want to know why I want to do my experiment?"

"I had a feeling that is what you were leading up to. Yes, why?"

"I don't think I will tell you until it's completed. I could be wrong about it. Let's talk about celibacy."

"Let's hear it."

"Okay," said William. "One of the lamest excuses I hear for not allowing priests and nuns to be married is the job is too difficult or too important. Brain surgeons, airline pilots, astronauts, physicists or engineers can be married. Nobody questions their ability to perform their job. It's ridiculous. I am going to advocate their marriage if they desire. St. Peter even took time to cure his mother-in-law and he still did a good job, didn't he?"

"William, it is a rule."

"It is a man-made rule. Notice I use the word 'man'. In the early days the Church worried about beneficiaries. They didn't want the priest, bishop or pope to hand down church possessions or artifacts or, God forbid, the Church treasury. And finally, they feared nepotism and rightly so. It occurred multiple times in our early Church History."

"Where did you read that?"

"Go ahead, Peter. Deny it. Deny there was no nepotism in our early history. Also deny the early Church leaders forced the children of early married popes be turned into the streets or orphan homes. The mothers of these children were made destitute. Some even died. "

The Cardinal remained silent.

"You know how I can prove the man-made rules aren't handed down by God?"

Cardinal Icarcion said, "Okay. I suppose you're going to tell me. How?"

"Our Church Fathers have never altered or modified any of God's Ten Commandments. They wouldn't dare. But they have changed and supposedly perfected most of the Church's man-made commandments. Is that not true?"

Cardinal Icarcion sat silently for a moment. "We simply interpreted them so the laity could understand them."

"Oh come on, Redaro. There's that word interpret again. You Cardinals use that interpret word like a defensive weapon. I'm not buying it."

"Your Holiness," said Cardinal Icarcion. "It seems to me you just want to tear the Bible apart. Everything written in the Bible according to you is interpretation, not inspiration. Are you saying everything is not as written, only as some writer made his own elucidation? If that be true, then the whole Bible can be thrown out and we can make our own rules. Is that what you want?"

"No, no, Redaro," said Pope William. "Not the whole Bible. Just a very, very few things seem to not make sense. What I am trying to say is a human hand put down what he interpreted as God's word. The problem is language. Sometimes the language in use at the time doesn't have a proper word. There are remote tribes having ten different words for the color of blue. There may be poor choices for a certain word the writer desires, so he does the best he can. Then someone else has to decipher it to change it to the language he's translating to. This can happen over and over again down through the centuries. So what I'm saying, we have to add common sense to these translations. Then some Church leader wants to change the words to his beliefs, for example, sex is vile. Do you see where I'm going with this?

Cardinal Icarcion again was lost in thought for a moment. "I don't like to think in that manner. I am very comfortable with my religion as is. I don't want to upset my beliefs. As you Americans say, I am warm and fuzzy with my faith. Don't change it."

"Redaro, can I say it any plainer? The Bible has undergone hundreds of reinterpretations, redefinitions and retranslations with thousands of footnotes and explanations. All these vicissitudes were performed by humans, not God. The inspirations were by God but humans put it on paper. And I repeat for the umpteenth time, was this kind of interpretations done to the Ten Commandments?"

Cardinal Incarcion said nothing.

"Cardinal, you must try to stay relevant to your people. Those that stand still are moving backwards."

The Cardinal looked downcast.

CHAPTER TWENTY-ONE

After six months as head of over a billion Catholics, Pope William found himself appreciably accepted as St. Peter's successor. His trial celibacy edict took a hit with the elderly clergy and it was what was expected. They fought it but Pope William said it was probably because they were too old to participate, or in other words, find a mate. Pope William and Peter thought it amusing. The laity and younger clergy readily accepted it. Everyone agreed it might reduce the sex scandal dilemma, not just with children but with adult members of the congregation, too. William did, however, have to repeat over and over again that celibacy of the clergy was an unwritten rule and not required in the early centuries. At first the Cardinals and bishops were preparing a retort. Within a month the canon lawyers did confirm William could over-ride their opinions and they dropped their objections.

After waiting a month, Pope William could wait no longer. He issued the Celibacy Edict against Cardinal Whittier's desire to have William wait a little longer.

A good result of the relinquishing of the celibacy requirement was the fact that many married deacons suddenly began to request continuing their studies toward priesthood. They desired to enter the priesthood, even more so than unmarried priests desiring to marry.

The world tour took Pope William to greet millions of the faithful. The majority of Catholics readily received him as Jesus's ruler on Earth with few exceptions. Meanwhile, Cardinal Perez has been fervently working with Detective Candelo. The detective feels he'll soon have an answer. Cardinal Perez is having some reservations. He feels the detective is possibly padding his fee and dragging his feet. A maid told Rosalie they heard Cardinal Perez yelling into a phone, "What's taking you so long?" and slammed the phone down. Rosalie explained to William the maid felt he was talking to Mr. Candelo.

Cardinal Whittier complimented Pope William on his fielding of a question asked by a woman regarding what form of birth control the Pope and his wife used. The Pope said it wasn't too difficult since as a policeman, especially as a rookie, he had to spend many hours on night duty. The rhythm method was rather easy to practice. In later years Rosalie had to have a hysterectomy.

Charles and David are fully involved in soccer. Charles has completely forgotten about football and his coach says he has a real talent for Europe's favorite game. The boys are constantly seen kicking a soccer ball around the Vatican. The Vatican gardener has had to repair several plants damaged by an errant kick here and there. The Swiss Guards, young deacons and priests were eager to participate and added to the damage.

Pope William called Cardinal Whittier into his office. "Peter," said William, "here's what I want. I want twenty men and twenty women for an experiment."

"William, you've been pestering me about this grouping for months. What for?"

"I don't want to tell you now but you can watch."

In the past six months, the Cardinal has acquired the habit of rolling his eyes heavenward. "Okay, William. What is it?"

"I want the men gathered in the Sistine Chapel first and the women there the next day. I want a good cross section of people; religious, laborers, business people, teachers and even atheists. I would like them to be fluent in English too. Make it as good a variety as possible, old and young. Hopefully they won't all be Italian. Mixed races, too."

The Cardinal smiled. "When?"

"As soon as possible. This has been bothering me for years."

"Really?"

"Since high school," said William.

"You amaze me, William. You amaze me."

"Sometimes I amaze myself."

"What's going to happen?"

The Pope picked up a folder. "I'm going to present them a scenario. I am going to verbally give them a scene and then they are going to write their version of what they heard."

"William, as a police officer, did you have to listen to two or more different versions of an accident or robbery?"

"Exactly. That's where I got the idea."

Again the Cardinal gave an exasperated look toward heaven. "William, what are you going to do with the results of your experiment, although I shudder to imagine."

William smiled, "That my good Cardinal is where your patience will be tested.

"Okay, William. I'll set it up in five or six days. I can hardly wait."

"Fine. Now. What's the latest on Cardinal Perez?"

"I've heard through the grapevine Josip expects a report from his detective friend this month. I personally think detective Candelo is a slacker but that's Josip's problem. I also heard he is livid regarding your celibacy memo. Between you and me, and this is not too Christian of me, I heard a young seminarian say Josip hates the idea because he is too old and ugly."

"I wish he could be a little open minded about these changes. Peter, if it turns out I was falsely elected, what will happen to me? What will happen to the Church?"

Peter looked out the window. "If the election was not concocted by you, you will be quietly sent back to Peoria. And if I were you, I'd then quietly move to Alaska. The Church on the other hand will elect a new pope and who knows what he'll do?"

"Peter, I honestly didn't instigate this."

"I know, William."

"Thank you."

"William, I hate to add this to your problems but there is a nun in New York. She is very vocal and very intelligent - and a very good Catholic. She has been banging on our door for the last several years to have a private audience with the Pope. Now you're the Pope so she feels you'll be in her corner."

"As if I didn't know, what does she want?"

"To put it simply, to be ordained."

William said, "I think by now you know how I feel about the ordination of women but I'm not ready to bring that theory to light. I have not made a final decision yet, but I can tell you this. My little experiment will help me considerably."

"I sorta thought that."

"Do you want to see Sister Ann before or after your experiment?"

"Immediately after I present my results to the College of Cardinals and the Roman Curia. I might add, Peter, the results won't have an immediate effect on my judgment. It'll just be further considerations for me."

Cardinal Whittier said, "I am thankful you're not taking this challenge lightly."

"I don't want to make it too easy for Cardinal Perez."

"I agree," said the Cardinal. "Oh, here's a new problem for you. A man in Japan is declaring the Blessed Virgin appeared to him. He was watching CNN and suddenly there she was, in living color. CNN took it somewhat seriously and said they had no word of any satellite interference world-wide."

"You know, Peter. The first tendency is to laugh it off but I guess it is not the Christian thing to do. Why is it so easy to be uncharitable?"

"It is always amazing to me how quickly those so-called events gather a following. He's already raked in a month's salary. His local parish priest is meeting with him next week. He'll report his findings to us. The man is asking you to declare him a saint. He seems to have as many followers as detractors."

Pope William asked, "What about that girl declaring she is having a virgin birth?"

"She confessed. Her boyfriend was not St. Joseph – nor the Holy Spirit. It was a school friend."

"One less problem for me."

"I'll have your experiment set up for Monday. Now let's dispense these problems to the Cardinals I have indicated."

"By the way," said Pope William, "where is this Sister Ann?"

"She is staying here in the Vatican until she has an audience with you. She has made herself quite useful, though. She's assisted with several work-shops regarding health care for the elderly."

"Good Lord! Tell her I'll see her tomorrow."

"Okay, you asked for it, or her."

Pope William didn't know what to expect from Sister Ann. Her appearance was what he expected, though. She was a matronly woman but not bulky. She appeared about fifty, no wrinkles, no glasses and about five and a half feet tall. She was dressed in ordinary women's clothes and the only way you would know she was a nun was the large crucifix on a sturdy chain around her neck. Her piercing blue eyes told Pope William this was a no nonsense woman. She looked William straight in the eye. "Your Holiness," she said. Then she whipped off her coat and knelt before the pope. Having met several Popes, this was the first Pope she met near her age.

"Sister Ann," said William. "I've been Pope for six months and I still don't know if I should be addressed as 'Your Holiness' or just plain William. You know I am not ordained. Anything holy I might do is orchestrated by Cardinal Whittier seated here."

The Cardinal nodded to sister, "Hello, Sister," he said.

The nun acknowledged him. "No matter, you are my Pope. I truly believe it was a miracle that God elected you. I feel you are a man our Church truly needed."

Pope William said, "I know your reason for being here and I hope you are not patronizing me."

"Your Holiness, I like your get to the point attitude. Surely you know my background and it must be very obvious why I am here. I won't waste your valuable time. Will you see to it that women can be ordained?"

"Wow," said William. He was taken by surprise. "You do get to the point."

Sister Ann smiled. 'Why waste time beating around the bush?"

"Sister, have you studied the impediments to ordaining a woman? Have you read the past history of Catholicism and where women have been placed in the Church? You know the obstacles?"

"I do."

"Let me restate the biggest and most formidable," said William. "And call me William."

"Yes, William."

"As if you didn't know, this place is run by old men, or in other words a 'good ol' boys' club."

"I am very aware of that," said Sister.

"Can I trust you to keep a secret?"

"No."

"Good," said a smiling William. "I am in your corner. I see no reason to keep women out of priesthood. But, and it's a tremendous 'but', it will take a wholesale change of the guard. This good ol' boys club has been entrenched for centuries, even before Christ was born. You know yourself, women were expected to bare children, cook food and be available for sex. That was it. I truly would like to break the stained glass ceiling of the Roman Catholic Church."

Sister Ann said, "My goodness. I love that phrase 'stained glass ceiling'. My I use it?"

"Surely. Now that you know my predicament, what do I do?"

Sister Ann was silent for a moment. "Can't you just do it? Just say women can be ordained?"

"Sister, you know better than that. We'd lose half of our members, especially the elderly."

"I know. I was being facetious. I guess I'm not too sure how it should be accomplished. I suppose I am one of those people pointing out a problem with no idea of a solution."

"That's my dilemma. Sister," Pope William paused, "What do you do in New York?"

"I teach in a college."

"Could you get some time off?"

"To do what?" the Sister asked.

Pope William paced the room. "As you know, I was a policeman in Illinois. By the way, did you know Pope Benedict XVI was the son of a policeman? Also the title of Pope didn't even exist until the fourth century. Allegedly the Papal oath didn't exist until the twelfth century and there's doubt it even did exist. Supposedly modern day Popes don't recite the oath. It has to do with a currant day Pope forbidden to change any teaching by a previous Pope. No one asked me to recite the oath."

"I wasn't aware of that."

"Sister,I am not a learned man. The only religion teachings I had were in parochial schools. It wasn't much. I have plenty of male advice but no female on my staff. Cardinal Whittier and I know we have very strong enemies here in the Vatican. They are attempting to force me to resign or at least prove a diabolic maneuver placed me here. Any move to bring the Roman Catholic

Church to contemporary times will be resisted by my enemies. In other words, I may not be Pope long."

"Gracious, are the enemies that prevalent?" asked Sister Ann.

The pope motioned to Cardinal Whittier. "Tell her, Peter."

"If you remember your history of the early Church then you know there were many rumors of unpopular popes being poisoned. A false rumor existed for a while that Pope John XXXIII's life was malevolently shortened. It was later determined correctly that he was fighting a losing battle with stomach cancer. He tried some unpopular actions to modernize the Church..." The Cardinal stopped speaking.

"Your Holiness, are the feelings that strong?"

"Very," said William. "What I am getting around to is I need a female voice. I need a very educated female voice."

Sister Ann laughed. "Now who is patronizing?"

"Could you spare six months or more to work with me? It might be even remotely hazardous."

"What would you have me do?"

"I need facts. I need examples - or lack thereof - where the Bible speaks of the role of women in the Church. I want to show these detractors there is no direct scripture saying women can't be ordained, or where it is even inferred. Cardinal Peter knows the Bible quite well for my use but he knows it from a man's viewpoint. I need a woman's viewpoint."

Sister thought about it a minute. "I guess I could but I am truly flattered. I didn't expect this."

"You would be working with several Canon Lawyers. Don't worry. They are on our side."

Cardinal Whittier said, "I would notify your superior."

"Sister Gretchen will be stunned to say the least."

William stood up. "Cardinal Whittier and Father Theil will be our coordinating personnel. The two Cannon Lawyers are Cardinal Larenzo and Cardinal Romando. I believe we'll make a good team but we will have to keep a very low profile for now. Agreed? "

"Definitely."

"Sister Rose William will find you quarters and Peter will communicate to your superior. Are we set?"

Everyone agreed.

"Oh. I'd like to meet your wife," said Sister. "Is she available?"

"Yes. She's in the next room." William called her. "Rosalie, Sister Ann would like to meet you."

Rosalie came in the room. "Rosalie. This is Sister Ann from the States."

"Hello Sister. I heard you've been in Rome for a while waiting to see my husband."

Sister said, "Yes but I've kept busy admiring the gardens."

"They're beautiful but there's a problem. I've been meaning to talk to you, William. It's the boys," said Rosalie.

"What's that about?"

Rosalie said, "It seems Charles and a new seminarian, Dominic, are complaining that the Vatican grounds are half garden. They said the Columbus Pius XI soccer field is always busy. He said all this flower stuff is a waste and they want to convert some of it to another soccer field, at least to a half soccer field."

Sister Ann burst out laughing.

"Oh, Lord," said the Pope. "You mean the big field is always crowded?"

"Charles said the seminarians and deacons are practicing for the next two or three months for the up-coming Clericus Cup. Even the FIFA and UEFA know about it. There is even a cute little grandstand that overlooks the field with the Basilica in the background. Charles said Dad's the boss. Can't he just command it to be converted."

"Okay. I'll have a talk with Charles, and who's this seminarian Dominic?"

"I don't know but I'll find out."

"As you can see, Sister," said Pope William. "It's still a normal family, almost."

"Thank you for seeing me, your Holiness," said the Sister as she rose to leave. "I'll keep in touch. Let me know how the soccer field turns out. Do they play in this cold weather?"

"Yes they do and I'll let you know about the soccer field."

"Charles said they could get it ready by spring," said Rosalie.

CHAPTER TWENTY-TWO

A cold winter morning found Pope William and Cardinal Whittier in an even colder Sistine Chapel. Lenten services were in full swing. Several other Cardinals and priests were present for the experiment. A few nuns wanted to watch too. Everyone was extremely curious and even betting what Pope William had in mind. The Pope stood in front of the twenty men.

"Gentlemen," he said. "Here's what is going to happen. I am going to present a scene. It's about a family. There is a father, a mother and three children. There is also a hiker. The family is on a picnic. They are on a hillside overlooking the Mediterranean. The hill has a rather steep cliff down to the sea.

"The children's ages are ten, eight and about a year and a half. The parents are preoccupied with preparing their meal. The baby has crawled off toward the edge of the cliff. Eventually the toddler reaches the edge and is preparing to crawl farther out to pick a flower. The parents and other siblings do not see the baby.

"A hiker is coming on the scene and sees the baby reaching for the flower. Just as the baby begins to slip over the edge, the hiker grabs the baby and calls to the parents. They are ashamed that they had not been watching their child and thank the hiker profusely.

"What I want you to do is write a short summary of the story, giving names to the parents, the children, the baby and the hiker. Take your time."

Cardinal Whittier, and the others present looked at the Pope curiously. "Do you know what he's up to?" asked one priest.

"I am not sure but I bet it'll be startling."

"John," said Pope William, "would you pick up the papers when they are through? Peter, tomorrow we'll do the same with the women. Wednesday I'll read through them and have results for you to ponder."

Cardinal Whittier looked over to one of the other Cardinals present and said, "I'll say this. Pope William's papal reign sure isn't boring."

Cardinal Menzotti said, "After six months he still scares me."

William said, "Now I'll take these stories and analyze them. I won't present the results and what they mean until sometime later. Peter, very soon I want to call a council or convention or whatever it's called. I have my next project ready to present to the bishops and Cardinals."

"The best word is conference," said Cardinal Whittier.

The Pope thanked all the attendees and told them they will soon see the results and how he would like the results to affect his discussion on the readings of the Bible.

After the people left the Chapel, Cardinal Whittier took Pope William aside. "William, remember what I told you the other day? You have to admit, you have some radical ideas. In the Church at this time, we have some old bishops and Cardinals. More correctly, some are very old. My gut feeling is you are going to have some stiff resistance to your contemporary proposals. Fortunately, since you've been pope, a backlog of vacancies has built up. I say fortunately because you have the opportunity to appoint bishops and Cardinals who are younger and more likely to accept your modernizing and streamlining. With that in mind, let's fill our vacancies before we do much more. Let me sound out our choices of men who will lean our way. It's the way it has been done down through the ages. Are you okay with that?"

"Peter, you are my advisor. What you say makes sense. Let's get started. For some reason I feel my time as pope is limited."

"I didn't want to say it but I feel that way too, William. I hope this is what God had in mind when he appointed you as pope."

The two men left the cold chapel. "I worry about that every day," said William. "Let's make a list of vacancies and who we can appoint to fill them. What's the earliest we can have a conference?"

"It's best we give the Cardinals a month to arrange a trip here. There will be some grumbling but they'll be here, mainly out of curiosity. The bishops have to come to Rome every five years anyway. They were just here last year but we won't give them a choice."

"Can we have the new bishops and Cardinals in place soon, before the conference?"

"Yes," said Cardinal Wittier. "We'll start immediately."

CHAPTER TWENTY-THREE

Over one hundred Cardinals and bishops were gathered Monday morning for Pope William's conference. They all knew what was on the agenda; clergy celibacy. Pope William was armed with a plethora of notes from Sister Ann. While having little to do with the ordination of women, it had a substantial bearing on celibacy.

"Gentlemen, you know why we are gathered here. We have a discipline that is hindering our growth. Clerical celibacy is a discipline, not a doctrine. I am going to put an end to it. It is foolish and prevents the Catholic Church from evangelizing. In order to grow, we need more priests, brothers and nuns. In the past six months I have been reading a ton of material regarding celibacy. It has been a restrictive doctrine in effect for almost seventeen hundred years. There is nothing in the Bible demanding celibacy.

"Another point is sexual persuasion. I have had no education in psychology but in my opinion could our Church doctrine regarding celibacy give us the label as a haven for gays and lesbians? I can't say there is a connection but we're not going to ostracize those of different sexual persuasion. We must plainly explain their unusual place in Christ's Church. We have to accept gays and lesbians as full members into our Church but whether they can become priests, nuns or brothers is a question I can't answer without help from our canon lawyers."

Cardinal Perez stood up. "I am leaving!" Cardinals Peligrini rose too.

"I'd like to advise that anyone choosing to leave may end up being relived of any and all of their duties. I have already selected several new bishops and Cardinals and in the future, I will need more. As most popes have done, they select men of their way of thinking. You could call it stacking of the deck. If you want to have any input on the outcome of this conference, you best stay. At least you will have heard firsthand what was spoken. How will you know what to condemn of me if you don't know what I said?"

The two Cardinals sat down.

"Now, let me be perfectly upfront with you. I disagree heartily with celibacy for our clergy. It should be a choice, not a mandate. For the past six months I have combed the Bible and any other text relating to celibacy in the Church. There is no definitive statement demanding clerical celibacy. Can anyone here show me where celibacy is demanded in the Bible? Can anyone show me where celibacy has helped us gain clergy - and members - in our Church?"

Pope William could see several Cardinals squirming in their seats.

"There are so many ways to look at the celibacy issue," Pope William continued. "The Catholic Church has never taught that all clergy must be celibate. Eastern Catholic Churches, such as Byzantine have consistently had the option of married clergy. The West made it normative in A. D. 306 at the Council of Elvira and made in mandatory in1074 by Pope Gregory VII. The Second Lateran Council in 1139 reaffirmed it." The Pope ran his fingers through his graying hair. "Why am I reading these notes to you Church Scholars? You have studied Church history all your adult life. You know all these statistics. I've just taught a few Bible classes to some of my St. Sabina parish. The celibacy issue always comes up.

"To be fair with both sides of the question, I will read several lines from the Bible that I feel can be misconstrued to justify either sides of the equation. Let me restate, celibacy is a discipline, not a doctrine. In 1 Corinthians chapter 7:32-34, Paul says 'An unmarried man is anxious about the things of the Lord, how may he please the Lord. A married man is anxious about the things of the world, how may he please his wife, and he is divided. An unmarried woman or virgin is anxious about the things of the Lord, so that she may be holy in both body and spirit. A married woman, on the other hand, is anxious about the things of the world, how she may please her husband'. On the other hand, 1 Corinthians 9:5 states 'Do we not have the right to take along a

Christian wife, as do the rest of the apostles, and brothers of the Lord? And as I previously stated from Genesis 1:28 'God blessed them saying: 'Be fertile and multiply; fill the earth and subdue it.' That, gentlemen, is an opinion, not a directive.

"Yes, celibacy can have a positive impact on their ministry. The converse is also true. It can have a negative impact of his ministry. In Matthew 19:12 Jesus mentions some becoming 'eunuchs' for the kingdom of God. Celibacy is encouraged to a certain degree as I have said before. In other words, seeing to the needs of one another's spouse as I previously stated as St. Paul said in Corinthians. It is not required. The apostle Paul seems to assume bishops and deacons will be married, 1Timonthy 3:1-4 It states, **1** 'This saying is trustworthy: whoever aspires to the office of bishop desires a noble task. **2** Therefore, a bishop must be irreproachable , married only once, temperate, self-controlled, decent, hospitable, able to teach, **3** 'not a drunkard, not aggressive, but gentle, not contentious, not a lover of money. **4** He must manage his own household well, keeping his children under control with perfect dignity'.

"Why was celibacy officially required? It was because in the third century nepotism and the abuse of giving of Church property to descendants became rampant. Although not the first mention of celibacy, the Council of Elvira, A.D. 306 and Carthage A.D. 390 made it a requirement of the Church because of nepotism and no other reason. Nepotism even brought about unqualified leaders in the Church. In a book used to support the origins of priestly celibacy, Peter Fink of Catholic University used his analyses and his interpretations as reasons enough for celibacy. No facts. Just his reasoning. Nothing from the Bible was applied. Anybody want to argue that point with me?"

Cardinal Perez spoke up. "Your Holiness. I happen to know a few Bible verses myself. How about this? 1 Corinthians 7: 38. 'So then, the one who marries his virgin does well; the one who does not marry her will do better'."

"That may be true," said the Pope, "but once again, does it demand celibacy?"

No one spoke.

"Here's another point." Pope William fully expected an outcry. "Why is the Church so hung up on virginity? The litany says ad nausea regard Mary's virginity. For example, virgin most pure, virgin most chaste, virgin most undefiled, virgin most snow white. To that they add Joseph, her most chaste husband. Poor man. On December 8, 1854 Pope Pius IX suddenly declared he was infallible. He then declared Mary was a virgin before, during and after Christ's birth. In 1869 the first Vatican Council agreed with his infallible decision. Definitely Mary could be a virgin before Christ's birth if God desired and afterward, too, if He so desired. But it's in the Bible. Matthew 1:25 says 'He (Joseph) had no relations with her (Mary) until she bore a son, and named Him Jesus'." I believe the writer wanted to make sure all knew Joseph wasn't responsible for the conception of Jesus. That's how the Church explains it away. But isn't it laughable? If God made Jesus' birth a beautiful occasion, why would He want to hide it or say it was not a normal conception? I know the Greek word 'until' doesn't imply normal marital relations but neither does it exclude it. Sometimes I think you saintly, old men truly wished the stork brought beings into the world."

Cardinal Di Magio said, "You are using the word interpretation to you own advantage."

The elder Cardinal Madino asked, "What's this about a stork?"

Irritably Cardinal Perez said, "Graco, I think old age is catching up with you."

"I'll have more to say about interpretation in a minute," said Pope William, "but here's another verse from the Bible and I've quoted it before. In Matthew 13:55 says 'Is He not the carpenter's son? Is not His mother named Mary and His brothers James, Joseph, Simon and Judas? Are not His sisters all with us?' Then again in speaking of Jesus Luke 8:19:20 says 'Then His mother and his brothers came to Him but were unable to join Him because of the crowd. He was told, 'Your mother and your brothers are standing outside and they wish to see you'. Isn't it possible Joseph and Mary were not celibate? Where does the Bible say they were celibate? And would it be such a terrible thing if they were not celibate?"

"Simply misinterpretations," said Cardinal Di Magio. By 'brothers' they meant they were actually His disciples."

Pope William said, "Once again a convenient misinterpretation. Well then, how about the statement about his 'sisters'?"

"It doesn't mean sisters."

"Why not?" asked Pope William. "What does it mean?"

The Cardinal had no answer.

Pope William said, "It seems to me if a Biblical passage disagrees with your teachings you call it a misinterpretation but if it agrees with you, you call it a proper interpretation." Pope Willian added, "Let me add this, Giovanni. I want to be fair. I can see where confusion or interpretation can enter the scene. In Mathew 12:50, Jesus said, 'For whoever does the will of my heavenly Father is my brother, and sister, and mother'. It is repeated in Mark 2:35, [For] whoever does the will of God is my brother and sister and mother'. I am not saying it is or is not an article of Faith that Jesus had brothers and sisters. I am saying it is open to interpretation. God could definitely perform a miracle by having Mary be a virgin before and after Christ's birth. He can do all things."

"I'm going to see you are the first Pope excommunicated," said Cardinal Signorelli.

"Giovani, have you forgotten in our early Church history several Popes excommunicated each other? But to continue, how about this? Here is another way to look upon interpretation. As you most likely know, I performed an experiment last March. While not definitively proving my point about Biblical interpretation, it does reveal interpretation and what the press call spin. Let me detail the experiment and the conclusions of it."

After giving the contents of the experiment Pope William said, "I have placed before you the substance of the scenario I presented to the twenty men and twenty women I used in my experiment. The only person I was interested in was the hiker; the one who saved the baby, a savior so to speak. All of the men gave a male name to the hiker, the 'savior of the baby'. Every woman gave a female name to the hiker, the savior of the baby'. Does that surprise you? Now let's look at the writers of the Bible. They were all men. They were educated men. Were there any women writers? No. Why not? At that time women were not allowed to be educated. They could not read or write.

"Just for fun, let's say you were sitting at your desk. You suddenly had an inspiration to write of some incident. The inspiration was of the first being created by God. What sex would you give it? I am almost certain it would be a male creature."

A Cardinal yelled out, "God said it was a man!"

"How do you know for sure?"

"God said it!"

"I ask again, how do you know?"

"It was inspiration directly from God. I am leaving. This is heresy!" Cardinal Paulo still stood by the door.

"Don't you want to hear the rest of my thoughts?" said Pope William. "Remember what I told Josip? How can you condemn me of something if you don't know what it is?"The Cardinal returned and slowly sat down. "Don't misunderstand me. I not saying you have to believe it was any other being than a man. I am just asking the question and you can believe what you want. I've asked this question before, why is there always a vocal few of our aged Church leaders so insistent on practicing misogyny?"

"What does that mean?" asked Cardinal Bendido.

"Hatred of women," said Pope William.

Pope William added another thought provoker. "Let's ask another question. The Bible says God took a rib from Adam and created Eve. Does it make sense that after God created Eve, Adam traveled around with twelve ribs on one side and eleven on the other? What if the first human God created had both sex organs? I am not saying for a fact Adam had both reproductive organs, but only what if. The Bible says God saw he was lonely. How could he reproduce and fill the Earth? Was he supposed to mate with the animals? What if instead of a rib He then took the female organs out of Adam and created Eve? The men writing the Bible had no idea what organs the body contained, much less reproductive organs. Did all the animals already have both reproductive organs or did He have to take a rib out of each animal? Did God have to create a female animal for each creature? Did He create it out of the male species? These are questions you can ask yourself without blaspheming. Yes, God could definitely create a female species out of a rib if He desired. He could create her out of nothing if He so desired. Also, I am sure you learned men know of species of creatures on Earth containing both male and female reproductive organs. It's called hermaphroditism. Many varieties of earthworms, snails, sponges and lizards are such."

Cardinal Mancino said, "What's the purpose of this meeting?"

"The purpose is to show how Biblical interpretation should not affect our teachings of celibacy. Since the third century we have made it doctrine that the clergy must be celibate. Using the Bible, you can put your construal any way you want. Think Yolando, think. If God created only one human first, how could he reproduce? Even if he had both reproductive organs, he was alone. Doesn't that strike you as odd?

"My fellow religious," said the Pope. "Moses wrote of events that occurred centuries before he was born. Moses lived between 1500 BC through 1300 BC, yet he wrote of happenings that transpired from Adam and Eve. The accounts were handed down in stories, poetry and songs. There was no writing yet. We are told there was great detail and accuracy but it was not perfect."

"GOD GUIDED THEIR HANDS!" yelled Cardinal Paulo.

Pope William ignored the outburst. "The Ten Commandments were written on tablets of stone. That you cannot argue with. Until there were written words, everything else was passed on in traditional oral storytelling. I am sending my trial proclamation to all Cardinals, archbishops and bishops that could not attend today. I will ask if there are any concepts I have forgotten to think about. If they or you cannot bring forward any factors that I have missed, then I will issue the edict that celibacy is strictly optional."

A boisterous murmur rose from the gathered religious men. "You can't do this!" said a Cardinal.

Cardinal Perez said, "God will see that you will not live to proclaim this heathenistic proclamation." With that he stormed out of the room.

Cardinal Icarcion said, "The Pontiff and I have gone through this discussion before. You're not going to change his mind."

Cardinal Flanis said, "Why are you doing this? I have been backing you since your election but this is too argumentative. Do you truly believe it will bring our Church to contemporary times?"

"Ivan, I've had questions since high school about the lack of common sense in the Church's principles. I said over and over, why are we the way we are? Does the Church revel in the way they stick their nose in the air and simply say that's the way it is. It's almost as if we dare an interpretation other than what has been stated as doctrine. And not religious doctrine mind you, but from some interpretation by some religious translator. If anyone expresses doubt, they could be excommunicated. That doesn't make sense. I say again, the Bible does not require celibacy but only encourages it. Even Paul realizes most clergy will be married. How can you argue for celibacy with those facts in front of you?"

Cardinal Flanis and others stood up, preparing to leave.

Cardinal Lopez said, "Your Holiness, it seems to me you are trying to say the entire Bible is subject to human interpretation. Is that your intention?"

"Jose, isn't it true? Hasn't that been the case for centuries? Hasn't the Bible been interpreted down through the centuries and even today? Look at the millions of footnotes in your Bible now telling us what the writers really meant? Look how many times the interpretations have been modified. I believe God is amused by the way we've taken His inspirations and drifted off in diverse directions."

Cardinal Asanti said, "I have to admit, you've brought up concepts I haven't thought about. I truly hope God has a plan for you and us." With that the Cardinals left the room.

Pope William walked over to Cardinal Whittier. "Well, I've laid the groundwork," he said.

"You've got some pretty rough ground to traverse," the Cardinal said.

"I know but I had to get it out there sooner or later."

Cardinal Whittier said, "I applaud you for waiting this long. Let's see what happens."

"We can see if those young Cardinals and bishops we appointed can help."

"It reminds me of an old Chinese curse," Cardinal Whittier said. "May you live in interesting times."

"Amen," said the Pope. "I am going to pray."

"Me too."

CHAPTER TWENTY-FOUR

In the Vatican, the edict abolishing the requirement of clergy celibacy was agreed upon with less controversy than expected. Outside the Vatican, though, it was a different story. Much controversy arose but as time passed the disagreements seemed to die down. Cardinal Whittier entered the Pope's office.

"William," said Peter. "I have some good news and some bad news."

"Okay, only I want the bad news first."

The Cardinal shuffled some papers in his hands. "A few dioceses and their bishops have decided to declare your election invalid. They say you are not the legal pope."

"Where are they?"

"Two in South America, two in Europe, one in Canada and one in New York state. They are now commencing communication with each other and deciding how to elect what they call a legitimate pope. I fear there will be others."

"Wow!" said William. "Can this be done?"

"It's happened before," said Peter. "One pope's followers literally fought it out with the other pope's followers. There was a time, 304 to 306 AD when there was no pope at all and a time when there were two - even three - Popes. A story has it that woman was Pope for a short time although she hid her gender."

Several requirements were mandated before a priest was permitted to marry. Pope William and Cardinal Whittier agreed to a year studying the pros and cons of the edict before granting any marriages. Eventually a local archbishop would be able to sanction the marriage. Certain stipulations were placed upon the marriage. It had to do with inheritance, wills and endowments. Nepotism could be an unfailingly arising abuse. Different than children of popes years ago, no pope today could name his offspring as any type of cleric. Pope William and Cardinal Whittier expected a rush of marriage applications but it never appeared. They assumed most applicants were waiting to see how the celibacy edict was being received.

Cardinal Whittier said, "I expect the most requests we get for marriage will be from married deacons. Most of the deacons wanted to be priests in the first place but couldn't because of the celibacy requirement. Most deacons are older men and I think they will be good candidates for the priesthood."

Cardinal Whittier and Pope William sat in the pope's office. "Peter, all I am trying to do is make our Church more able to help others and concentrate less on bureaucracy and ideology. I don't want to change dogma or any well-established beliefs. I will not change God's commandments. If God desired a virgin conception of Jesus, He could do it. God is most powerful and can do any miracle He desires. I feel the latest miracle is me – a pope. I am reminded of a question a student asked of my theology professor in school. He asked if God could make two liters of water fit in a one liter jar."

"What was his answer?"

"He said theoretically He could by making the molecules or atoms intertwine with each other, just as one liter of water added to one liter of alcohol doesn't make two liters of liquid."

"It doesn't?" said Peter.

William laughed, "Did you miss that class? The molecules combine with some of the other molecules – or something like that. I don't remember exactly how it works. The result was a liquid less than two liters."

"I guess I was asleep."

"You know now what my most annoying issues are with the Church; confessions, celibacy and the role of women. We seem to have won the change of the confessional and I hope celibacy. We fought – and are still fighting – the acceptance of black men and male Hispanics and men of all other races. The Church has fought for acceptance of men of all races, too. Gosh, the Vatican is still fighting non-Italians being named pope. But what about women? We still treat them as the Arabs, Muslims and other near east and Middle East countries regard them. We treat a woman as a possession. I've told you my concerns. I want another conference, Peter. I want it soon. The grapevine has told me Josip is having a meeting with Mr. Edwardo Candelo soon."

"I know, William," said the Cardinal. "I hesitated to tell you that."

"Sister Ann is meeting with me tomorrow."

"Does she have any more good information for you, William?"

The Pope looked out his oversize and ornate window." I'm afraid not much. There is so much resistance from the old established Cardinals. She can't find any of the older Cardinals that will even discuss the ordination of women. At least the younger Cardinals and archbishops we have installed have agreed to spend some time with her. I think I will have to just bully it through. I'll prepare my women's ordination edict now that the celibacy edict has been published. We are gaining a fair amount of acceptance from the clergy outside of the Vatican regarding celibacy. As a matter of fact, some are completely overjoyed at the revision. It will take some work and I've scheduled several meetings with our Canon Lawyers regarding women's ordination. Again, the young ones seem receptive to it. Sister Ann's comrades are actually dancing in the streets even though they realize they'll be retired by the time the women's edict would ever take effect. It won't be an overnight happening. With the resistance we're meeting it may never happen. Sister realizes that. So, what's the good news?"

Cardinal Whittier seemed thoughtful. "I've heard from many of the religious around the world and they tell me it would be a great help in relieving the priest shortage. And, as I said, the younger Cardinals and bishops do not seem too resistant."

Pope William said, "I wonder if future historians will look upon this year the same as we looked upon the Church in the third and fourth century?"

"I expect so," said Peter. "They are already writing our history regarding priest's celibacy as a monumental moment. I never thought it would be accepted. Actually, if you think about it, the idea wasn't as foreign as it originally seemed."

"Yes, it seemed dead in the water and suddenly it seems to be headed toward approval without many revisions."

"Appointing Josip as one of your secretaries was a smart move, too."

"You should know the Italian saying; keep your friends close and your enemies closer. I'm going to prepare the edict now regarding the ordination of women. Want to help?"

"Glad to," said Peter. "I wouldn't miss it for the world."

The young pope looked at Cardinal Whittier. "Will you still be so eager to help when I am attacked regarding the women's issue?"

"I, and Cardinal Larenzo and Romando, will be there, you can be sure."

Pope William said, "I know it's going to be a quite volatile issue. When I think about it I just don't understand why our early clergy was so turned against women. Was it just remnants of primitive regards of the woman's place in society?"

Cardinal Whittier said, "It may be. Has Rosalie given you any thoughts regarding the woman's place in the Church?"

"Now that I think about it, she's been quite silent about the matter. Every once in a while I tease her about being the weaker sex. Then she surprises me by rearranging the furniture. She's pretty smart, though. She and her art teacher have had some go rounds. I don't understand art but she has explained to me how she and her teacher differ. They're both Italian. That should explain it."

"I can imagine she could be a little fiery."

"Rosalie has been very docile since we have been in Rome," said the Pope. "I think she realizes I have enough going on that I don't need any domestic turmoil."

"How about your sons?"

"They've been great, too."

"How about you?"

"Is my hair getting whiter?"

"Yes, whiter and thinner."

"Don't let me get stooped shouldered," said Pope William."

CHAPTER TWENTY-FIVE

To the Venerable Cardinals, Archbishops, Bishops, priests, Brothers and Sisters and all of Good Will. God created man and woman to live together on His Earth. The same is true of all creatures on Earth. Male and female were directed by God to join together to perpetuate life on His wonderful creation. They were to join together to fill all the spaces of the Earth. Humankind was to join together to rule over all lessor creatures, treating them justly and fairly. This was the directive handed down by God. Mankind, and womankind, were placed above all other creatures on His Earth. However, he did not place man above woman, or woman above man. They are equal in His sight. God did, though, have to design a way to bring new life into the world. A human had to be brought to life by another human. There had to be a birth canal. The human with the birth canal was called woman. This being was no more or less of importance in God's plan.

Celibacy, in other words abstinence from God's design to procreate His Earth, became a norm in the Catholic Church. Why? Why is abstaining from God's plan so much more desirable in the Church's rituals? Genesis 2: 18 The Lord God said: "It is not good for the man to be alone. I will make a suitable partner for him." Genesis 1:27-28 God created man in his image; in the divine image he created him; male and female he created them. God blessed them, saying: "Be fertile and multiply, fill the earth and subdue it. Have dominion over the fish of the sea, the birds of the air, and all living things that move on the earth." Genesis 2:20-23. The man gave names to all the cattle, all the birds of the air, and all the wild animals; but none proved to be the suitable partner for the man. So the Lord God cast a deep sleep on the man, and while he was asleep, he took out one of his ribs and closed up its place with flesh. The Lord God then built up into a woman the rib that he had taken from the man. When he brought her to the man, the man said: "This one, at last, is bone of my bones and flesh of my flesh; this one shall be called 'woman,' for out of 'her man' this one has been taken."

God has plainly directed male and female to be fertile and fill the earth. How is it then that the act of male joining with female became vile and despicable? God made the act therefore it cannot be despicable. How then is it that the pleasure from this act is loathsome? God made the act therefore it cannot be loathsome. How did this act become so disgusting to some in the Catholic Church? Humankind made it so abominable. So how did humankind make is so abominable? Satan. Just as Satan made humankind feel shame in the Garden of Eden, he has made the act of man and woman joining as one seem contemptible and shameful to everyone.

Let's look at nature. God made beautiful mountains and oceans for us to see and enjoy. Is it so wonderful to not look at them? Will there be a higher place in God's kingdom for the human not looking at his beautiful world? What's the goodness in not looking at God's creation?

God made appetites in us to assure we would eat nourishment. Will there be a higher place in God's kingdom for the human not taking nourishment? Causing the body to be weak and frail by not taking proper nourishment is not God's intention. Fasting is great, especially when done to honor God, but does that make eating less than honorable? Gluttony is bad. It is eating to excess and it is Satan tempting us to the sin of gluttony. The feeling of the pleasure of eating wasn't made evil by God or man. Satan did it.

The act of intercourse and its pleasure isn't bad or despicable. It too was made by God. I ask again, who made it bad? Satan by the temptations of adultery and fornication made it bad .What I am trying to illustrate is the joining of man and woman is no more or less wonderful than practicing celibacy. Remaining celibate is great when done so to honor God but so is marriage. The bringing forth a child is in itself a miracle. The couple is fulfilling God's command, "Be fertile." Early Christendom is in error to expound the virtues of celibacy while making those in Holy Matrimony feel less holy. It is a mistake to state over and over again the point that clerics should be celibate. There is no statement in the Bible denoting that fact. Therefore I am issuing this edict that priests, brothers and sisters may at their choosing decide if celibacy is their calling.

To further illustrate we can look at the New Testament. Clearly many of the early Church Leaders were married. For some unexplainable reason around the third century intercourse between a properly married man and woman became a stain on a religious minister. The pleasure of a man and woman became a sin. How can an act made by God become a sin? I repeat, surely an act of adultery is a sin but it is a sin brought about by humankind and Satan, not God. God made the act of eating a pleasure but it can become a sin of gluttony by humankind, not God. These appetites created by God are wonderful and necessary to maintain life and health but it is Satan who makes improper use a sin, not God.

The writings of the Church today seem to try to make us forget that many of our first leaders were married. They try to hide the fact that married clergy was commonplace. True, celibacy may have been recommended but not required. In Corinthians 7:32-34 I should like you to be free of anxieties. An unmarried man is anxious about the things of the Lord, how he may please the Lord. But a married man is anxious about the things of the world, how he may please his wife, and he is divided. An unmarried woman or a virgin is anxious about the things of the Lord, so that she may be holy in both body and spirit. A married woman, on the other hand, is anxious about the things of the world, how she may please her husband. Mat 19:11-12 "He (Jesus) answered, not all can accept this word (celibacy), but only those to whom it is granted. Some are incapable of marriage because they were born so; some, because they were made so by others; some, because they have renounced marriage for the sake of the kingdom of heaven. Whoever can accept this ought to accept it." Clearly, it is a choice between two miracles, not good and evil. I repeat, it is a free will choice of two wonders, not a free will choice of good and bad.

In Timothy 1:4-5 "A bishop (in the early Church meaning an overseer) must manage his own household well, keeping his children under control with perfect dignity; for if a man does not know how to manage his own household, how can he take care of the church of God?" Titus1:6 Even Paul, who never visited Crete, left this letter to Titus regarding appointing presbyters "on a condition that a man be blameless, married only once, with believing children who are not accused of licentiousness or rebellious." Here Paul and others assume most are married.

While celibacy for the sake of adding to the greater glory of God can be good, to forcibly direct it to all clergy may not always be admirable and in some cases may actually dissuade some away from the Roman Catholic Church.

Pope William

CHAPTER TWENTY-SIX

Pope William called Cardinal Peter into his office. Pacing the floor nervously he turned off the background music and held up two printed pages.

"Peter. I'm preparing my ordination of women edict. Would you mind listening to it for me?"

"You don't waste time, do you? Is this a trial edict?"

"Yes. I'm going to let the Cardinals and bishops here in the Vatican read it and give me their opinion. I will wait until I get some feedback before I send it out. I am also going to spend some considerable time praying."

"Sure. Let's hear it. I have to admit I knew this day was coming and I wasn't looking forward to it."

"Is it that bad?"

"William, I just don't know. The Reconciliation Edict and the Celibacy Edict were accepted. I repeat, church attendance is up as are results in the collection basket. Requests to enter the priesthood have greatly increased, too. So, if those edicts made it okay, who knows? This may make it too, but please don't send it out until we both study the criticisms from our local clergy."

"Here goes."

> *Dear brethren In Christ, again in a most humble voice I want to greet you with another edict I feel will enhance our Catholic faith. In my continued effort to bring our Church into the modern era but without stooping to the worldliness and sinfulness of it, my wish remains to lead it as Christ would have. This is another effort to bring evangelization to the forefront. In order to spread the word we need many to become*

missionaries. It's no different than ages ago when the Word needed to be spread about. As it has been said many times, there are many fields to be cultivated but too few laborers. I am trying to change that.

We have at our disposal many able and willing laborers anxious to go into the fields. Unfortunately we are not using them. Due to age old prohibitions, biases, restrictions and almost prehistoric discriminations we are wasting these laborers. These laborers are being held back, wasting a valuable commodity. They want to go eagerly to the fields and spread the word of God. Ask yourself, what would Jesus do? The Bible tells how He would use these laborers. He consistently worked with these laborers and spent much time with them. He loved them as we should love them. Our Church only gives these laborers busy work; clean the altar, iron our vestments, set up candles, and teach in our schools. They are held back by our 'good ol' boy's mentality. They are held back by a stained glass ceiling.

These labors as you can guess are women. They fervently want to work the fields. Look how many parishes require a priest to go from one church for a Saturday six o'clock Mass to another for a Sunday eight o'clock Mass and then to another for a ten o'clock Mass. The priests performing these tasks are human and they are wearing out. They are over-worked and fatigued. Many other denominations have used these zealous laborers with great success. Why not the Roman Catholic Church? There is no good reason to not ordain a woman.

Why do we hold the woman in restraint? Are we jealous of the female? Maybe we should be. All we men can do better is lifting a heaver box. Women are the only instrument created by God to bring new life into this world. Every one of us came here by means of a woman. Doesn't that mean something? Truth be known maybe the woman should be the one ordained and we men do the labor. Did you ever think of the fact that God stands next to a woman as she conceives new life while He creates a soul? We men could be on the Moon while this miracle occurs. The woman is a miracle worker. Why do we men hold them down? Many countries have a woman as the leader or president of their nation. There have been successes and failures, but many seem to have survived and even prospered. Looking at the failures, corruptions and scandals we have had throughout the centuries with men as leaders, we certainly could not have a more immoral history.

I hope with your acceptance of this edict I can change this ridiculous restriction. I pray to God I am growing our Church.

Cardinal Whittier, like so many times before, remained speechless.

CHAPTER TWENTY-SEVEN

Cardinal Perez sat in his office next to the Pope's office. He watched the tourists shivering in the Italian winter air. His new secretary, Father O'Rourke entered the room.

"Cardinal, a Mr. Candelo is here. He says he has an appointment." Father Lawrence O'Rourke was a handsome, dark Irishman, thirty-six years of age and lately a favorite and constant companion of Cardinal Perez.

"Yes he does. Send him in."

The young priest motioned for the detective to enter Cardinal Perez's office.

"What in the hell has taken you so goddamn long?" said a highly agitated Cardinal. "Come with me. Let's go into the other office."

"Hello to you, Mr. Perez,' said Mr. Candelo sarcastically.

"Do you know how much money you are going to cost me?"

Edwardo sat in one of the plush chairs, not waiting for the Cardinal to offer him a seat. "Do you care to know if I have spent your money wisely?"

"You're damn right I do."

"You sure don't speak like a holy man, Josip."

"Get down to business. Do you have any results?"

"You bet, preacher man."

Cardinal Perez almost screamed. "For Christ's sake, what have you found?"

"Sit down and I'll tell you." The detective handed Josip a large envelope. "Open it."

Sweating profusely, the Cardinal opened the envelope and took out some ballots. They were exactly like the ones the Cardinals use to elect a Pope. The Latin phrase '*Eligo in Summom*

Pontificem was printed plainly on the top of the ballot. The rest of the ballot was blank. Edwardo Candelo said, "Just like you guys did last year, sign some name with this pen and then write the name of someone you want to vote for. Vote for Mario Lanza and sign it Walt Disney. Then fold it and put it on the table."

Nervously the Cardinal did as he was told.

"Now take out another one and vote for George Washington and sign it Donald Duck. Fold it and take out one more, vote for Jesus Christ and sign it Maria Alberghetti."

Angrily Cardinal Perez said, "I hope this is proving something."

"It will, Josip. It will," said Edwardo. "Now, we'll wait about five minutes and you can unfold them and read them."

The Cardinal fretfully paced around the room. After five minutes he grabbed one of the ballots and unfolded it.

"OH MY GOD!" he screamed. "It's signed Cardinal Giovani Signorelli and he voted for Mussolini!"

"Open another one."

Hands shaking he grabbed another ballot. Opening it, he yelled, "It's signed Cardinal Karl Stanlove and he too voted for Mussolini."

"Want to try the third one?"

Hands still shaking the Cardinal took out another one. Almost laughing he read it. "It is signed Cardinal Josip Perez and I voted for Mussolini. It looks exactly like my handwriting. Laughing hysterically the Cardinal said, "Do you have any more of these?"

"There's about thirty more in the envelope."

"How was it done? How did you get each Cardinal's handwriting?"

"My man tells me that is the easy part. He can copy anybody's handwriting."

Cardinal Perez had an evil smile on is fat face. "How did you get my original writing to disappear?"

Edwardo smiled. "Easy. My chemists. On the ballot the Latin jargon was already permanently printed. Each ballot I gave you was a specially treated paper. Already written with a special ink was Mussolini and your signature, or somebody else's. That writing was invisible. The pen I gave you contained a chemically treated ink. Anything you wrote would disappear in about three minutes. For my demonstration I supplied my chemist with samples of most of your cardinal buddy's signatures. I must add getting those samples cost me plenty in bribes. When you folded the ballot, we had the stuff we had previously written, like your Cardinal's forged names and Mussolini, appeared after five minutes. With a sample of anybody's handwriting my guys can easily reproduce any signature."

"What if I noticed my signature was disappearing on the ballot I signed? What if I noticed it changing into some other Cardinal's signature?"

"You would just assume no one would reopen their folded ballot once they folded it. Your guys up front would be the first to open a ballot. Yes, it would be a bit of a gamble but it could be done. The hardest part of this show would be setting it up with special pens and the special ballots ahead of time."

Rushing to his desk, the Cardinal unlocked a drawer. He took out an envelope and tossed it to the detective.

"Don't you want to hear the rest?" said the detective. "There's a little something strange, though."

"No! And since I am going to show this to the world there's no need to try to blackmail me. I will prove to the world that the great Pope William is a fraud. I will show the world exactly what you showed me. You could say it is great advertising for you. I don't care what you say. I am overjoyed."

"Okay," the detective said in a slightly dubious voice. "I was not able to find out who did it, though. I'm still working on that."

"FORGET IT! I DON'T CARE! This is all I need. I'm not paying you any more money."

"Okay."

"There's more than enough money in there. Take it and get out of here. I don't want to ever see you again!"

The big man counted the money and was satisfied. "A thank you Edwardo would be nice."

"GET OUT!"

"Sure, sure. See you in church."

Cardinal Perez had Father O'Rourke show the man out.

"Lawrence, this is the news we've been waiting for."

"Has he found the results you've been wanting?"

"Yes, Lawrence. Come and sit down here. We have to figure out how to use this information to get this imposter out of Rome. We will dispense the results slowly and at the right time. We will do it just before he issues his edict that women can be ordained. My informants have told me it's coming. Oh, I can't wait to see the expression on his face. And on that idiot Whittier. Larry, this calls for a toast of a favorite wine I have been saving for some great occasion such as this." Josip went to a locked cabinet to his left. "Here. It's a 1923 Fonseca Port. See. It's turned slightly amber from age but it brings out additional flavors. Let's have a great time tonight and tomorrow we'll decide how to use our ...let's call it evidence of deceit.

"Josip," said Father O'Rourke. "This is great news. Show me how it was done."

"Not now. Come here." Cardinal Perez put his arm around the priest's shoulder. "Lawrence, I'll tell you a little secret. I am going to be Pope very soon. I am going to be the first Pope from my country. As soon as William resigns, and I know he will, I can be elected Pope."

"This is truly a joyous occasion," said the priest. Looking at the ballots on Josip's desk he asked, "Are these the ballots?"

"Yes."

"How much did this cost?"

"Plenty but it was worth it, every penny."

"Can't you show me how it was done?"

"Yes, but I can't show you how right now. I only have thirty-five or more ballots. I don't want to waste any. I'm going to need all for my great display. Oh, the joy!"

Father O'Rourke asked, "Did he find out who did it?"

"No and I don't care.

CHAPTER TWENTY-EIGHT

Charles, David and several young seminarians noisily traipsed into the room. It was the middle of the afternoon. "Mom," said David. "Have you seen the Fountain of Galera? It's a giant model of ship with working water cannons."

"I know. I've seen it. I hope you boys didn't get in the water?"

"We thought about it but it was too cold. Oh, and did you know Pope Leo X had a pet elephant? It was a gift from the King of Portugal. It was buried under the parking lot by the Belvedere Courtyard. They found the bones when they were doing some plumbing work. And Dominic said that there's a hole in the wall of that tower that Pope Gregory XIII's astronomers used track the sun's movement and corrected the calendar. It was eleven minutes off per year."

Rosalie said, "That Dominic is a trove of information."

"Anyway we want to go over to Gabriele Bonci's Pizzarium. Can I drive?"

"You don't have a license yet. Anyway it's only five minutes away. You fellows can walk. I'm afraid you'll run over some tourists. The Square is always crowded."

"But Mom. Dominic is eighteen and he'll be with me. I have my *foglio rosa* permit – and I'm sixteen now. It's cold outside. There aren't too many tourists."

"Mrs. Meier," Dominic said, "There's too many of us for one auto. I'll ride with David and make sure he obeys the signs. Charles will drive the other auto."

"Can't you tremendously athletic soccer players walk for five minutes?" asked Rosalie.

"We're too tired, Mom."

"You boys do look a little ragged. Okay, but I'm putting you in charge, Dominic. Charles, make sure David uses his head - and seat belt. Remember, we are only temporary citizens of Italy. Don't create a scene. And use the Saint Anne's entrance. I don't want you boys to run over any visitors."

"Sure, Mom. Oh, the Clericus Cup is coming up soon." With that the boys were off.

"I know. When is it?" Rosalie asked. Too late. The boys were out the door.

Abruptly Charles stuck his head back in, "Mom, Dominic said I might make the Vatican Team!" With that he was gone again.

Cardinal Perez briskly walked into Pope William's office. "Hello, your Holiness," he said in an unusually cheerful tone. "Your speech about the abandoned children in Africa was most moving."

"Thank you," said Pope William. Praise from the Cardinal was most unusual.

"Any communiques you want me to answer today?"

"Just one extremely unusual one from your home country, Josip," Pope William noticed the change of mood. "It seems a lady wants her pet dog to receive Holy Communion."

"My goodness," Josip said. "There seems to be no end to the stupidity of some of our flock."

"You're right, Josip, but we have to remember they are all God's children and we have to respect everyone's wishes even though we may feel they are foolish."

Sitting in a comfortable couch, Cardinal Perez looked the Pope in the eye. "William, I need an unusual favor of you."

"Sure, Josip. What can I do for you?"

"William, I know you are the one who calls all the Cardinals and Bishops in for conferences and I have no right to but I have a very important statement to deliver to all."

"What is it about?" said William. "Last year with the confusion in the Conclave, my election and how it happened caused the Cardinals to remain in Rome a long time before they could return home. There was some grumbling and I don't blame them." Pope Whittier's spies had informed the Pope of the detective's recent visit to Cardinal Perez. "Does this have anything to do with your detective friend?"

"This is just a small matter that I think all the Cardinals and archbishops might like to hear. It is only a small matter to do with your edict on celibacy." The Cardinal was careful to not say yes or no. Stating it had to do with celibacy, though, was a lie.

"I don't know if I need more justification than what you gave me. Let me talk to Peter. He will know what it takes to call a special conference, and you're quite experienced in such matters. You should know too what it takes."

The Cardinal began nervously looking around, avoiding eye contact with the Pope.

"Josip, I was a policeman for quite a few years. One thing I learned was how to tell when someone is lying." Pope William let the sentence hang in space. There was a long pause. William said nothing, waiting for Josip to speak.

"Goddamn it! I know you are a fraud and I can prove it!" Cardinal yelled.

Ever softly William said, "Why didn't you say so. Yes. I'll call a special conference for you. It'll take several months to get everyone on board and make travel arrangements but I'll do it for you. You're aware we've just had a special conference. May I ask a question?"

"Yes!"

"Am I a fraud?"

"You know goddamn right you are!"

"Thank you. I'll start the proceedings right away. It may take until this summer, you know."

"Don't stall me! I need the meeting this month," said the Cardinal, voice still raised.

"I can't. You know that."

The short Cardinal looked around the room. "By damn, I'll find a way." Cardinal Perez knew he couldn't call an official conference but he could request a meeting and the Cardinals could agree to meet or not. Most assuredly all would not attend since the Cardinal wasn't as popular as he thought he was.

"May I hear what your friend has found in his discovery?"

"You can rot in Hell which is what you deserve."

"Good day, Josip."

Cardinal Josip Perez rose and left William's office with a satisfied grin.

Pope William paced the room. He entered Father Thiel's office and asked, "John, would you call Peter and ask him to come over here as soon as he has time?"

"Sure, your Holiness. I didn't like the look on the Cardinal's face as he left. I hate to meddle but did he have bad news?"

"John, I think the end of Pope William's reign is in sight."

"Oh no," was all the priest could say.

"See if you can locate Rosalie. She should be here too."

It was about four in the afternoon when Rosalie rushed into the Pope's office. Cardinal Whittier was already there.

"Bill, what is it?"

"It looks like the end of my reign is approaching. I was just filling in Peter. Cardinal Perez came in my office, just beaming. He just had a visit with his detective. I can imagine what it was about."

Rosalie sat down heavily on the couch. "Oh, Bill. I knew it was too good to be true. I was so looking forward to our first year here. The boys and I were just beginning to fit in." Tears were welling up in her eyes.

Cardinal Whittier said, "Now wait, Rosalie. We don't know for sure what Josip is going to say."

Rosalie said, "What else could make him so happy? At first I didn't want you to be Pope and now I love our life here. Oh William. What will we do if you're removed from your position? Where will we go? How will we live?"

"Easy now, Rosalie," said William. "Let's cross those bridges when we get to them."

"That's right, Rosalie," said Peter. "God will take care of you and your family."

"What he wants Peter, is for me to call a conference of all Cardinals and Archbishops as soon as possible. I told him most conferences were held usually every five years. He told me it was too important to wait. I assumed I might as well agree to it. As he left the room I asked him if I am a fraud. In no uncertain terms, in quite colorful words, he said yes."

"William, we know you are not a fraud. We don't know how it happened but you are not a fraud."

"I know he wants to call the conference before my edict on the ordination of women gets published. Peter, if he has definite proof that my election was fabricated, I will have to resign. "

Cardinal Whittier stood up. "I can understand that but I hope it doesn't come to that. My feeling it was a miracle was becoming stronger as the days and months went by.

"I wonder how the trial edict regard women's ordination is being considered by those here in the Vatican?"

"I was preparing to inform you on the results of it."

"I hate to ask."

"So far, quite favorable. The younger clergy are in favor of it and women are ecstatic. As you could have expected, word has leaked out beyond Vatican walls."

"Do I want to rush the final edict forward before the conference? I suppose I could stall the conference. He can't circumvent me, can he?"

"He could request a conference but the Cardinals wouldn't have to abide by his wish. He's not a real popular Cardinal."

Rosalie said, "I don't feel well. Bill, we couldn't go back to Peoria. I couldn't stand the shame."

Cardinal Whittier put his arm around Rosalie's shoulder. "There's no shame, Rosalie. William didn't do anything wrong."

"I won't rush the edict, Peter. Maybe God doesn't want women to be ordained. Maybe God never did want me to be Pope."

"William, let's wait and see what Josip presents. I am really curious what Josip's detective found out. I wonder if Josip will give us an advance explanation."

"No way. He told me in no uncertain terms I'd have to wait until the proper time."

"William," said Cardinal Whittier. "Let me think about this and get some advice. I will set up the conference for five months from now. Will you publish your edict regard women's ordination before the conference?"

William walked over to Rosalie and gave her a hug. "No. There is no use. As they say, it's dead in the water. How will it look if I send out the edict just as I am about to resign? Maybe the next Pope might want to try to follow through with it if the results continue to be favorable – that is if he's a young Pope. Maybe one of those younger Cardinals we installed might be elected Pope."

"William," said Cardinal Whittier, "Let's say it wasn't a miracle. Do you have any idea who could have done this? An enemy from back home?"

"No one of any importance."

Father Thiel entered the room. "Your Holiness, if I may say something?"

"Sure John."

"I heard a rumor going around some of the seminarians."

"What is it?" asked Cardinal Whittier.

"Cardinal Perez is lining up support for him to be the next Pope."

Cardinal Whittier said, "Oh my god. What arrogance. He'll never get close."

"You know, Peter," said a seemingly defeated Pope. "I don't care. I guess I always knew I shouldn't be here. I love my Church. I love my Catholic Faith. It's just I saw it losing members. I saw it losing relevancy. Young adults were flocking to other denominations and not to Catholicism. I guess I fell in love with my ideas. I suffered the sin of self-importance."

"William, don't beat yourself too much. Judging by the acceptance of the changes in reconciliation and celibacy I think you've done a world of good for our faithful. Nearly all dioceses world-wide have reported an upturn in attendance and in monetary support. I think God is satisfied with your mission. We'll have to see what happens on your next issue. So far there have been no schisms."

"Peter, we have to get the conference set up before five months. Rosalie and I cannot hang around in suspense that long. I'll go crazy."

"Okay," said Peter. "I suppose this is a critical enough situation we – you- can call an immediate conference. I'll help you. We'll explain the dire nature of the situation and call everyone in. We'll let them know it has to do with your reign. That should get their attention."

"Thank you, Peter."

Rosalie sat sobbing in the back of the room.

"I'll demand it be held next month. I imagine even Josip will help with the arrangements."

With that, Peter and John left William's office. Rosalie and William sat arm in arm in their cozy loveseat they brought to Rome from Illinois.

"William," said Rosalie. "What will we do? Did you do something illegal?"

"Rosalie, how can you ask that question? You know me better than that."

"I thought I knew you but now there is a doubt."

"Rosalie," William said even louder. "Why would I do something like this? Please, don't you doubt me. I need you on my side. Please, I know I was getting a little arrogant but I don't know how this happened."

Rosalie left the room sobbing quietly. Pope William sat alone in his office. He again read his copy of his trial edict regard women's ordination in almost a whisper.

The young Pope crumpled up the printed copy and threw it in the waste can. He thought about deleting his file copy on his computer but decided to do that tomorrow.

CHAPTER TWENTY-NINE

Five weeks have passed since Cardinal Perez made his request for a special conference. It will not be a Conclave, only a conference to discuss an important matter. If a Conclave is needed to select a Pope, it will be held almost immediately after the conference.

All the invited clergy are present and are awaiting Cardinal Perez to commence his conference. Strict instructions have been given to the Swiss Guards to allow none of the press or any of the public to enter the Basilica. Even the staff had to be kept away. Due to the great expanse of the Basilica it was fairly difficult to be absolutely sure no one other than Perez's invited guests was present.

Some of the Cardinals and archbishops have grumbled about having another meeting so soon but most are very curious about its content. Rumors have circulated about its substance but Cardinal Perez has been incredibly secretive about it. Some feel it has to do with the Pope's health. Cardinal Perez has been most religious and blatantly pious in his manner, visibly praying in a most obvious way. Cardinal Whittier said he is reminded of the Pharisees in the Bible and their outward pretense of holiness. Cardinal Perez has confided to those Cardinals of like mind that he feels if William resigns he should be immediately elected as the next Pope.

Pope William hasn't been seen in public since his meeting with Cardinal Perez. Cardinal Whittier has begged him repeatedly to no avail to make some appearances around the Vatican. Rosalie has been bringing his meals to his room where they have been eating alone with the two boys. Charles and David have lost their youthful exuberance and their soccer ball remains untouched. A depressing pallor hangs over the Meier family and the mood is affecting the Vatican staff. No one is sure what the problem may be but it is a sudden change to the mood of weeks ago. Sister Ann has tried repeatedly to see the Pope but William has refused to see her.

After several attempts to meet with Pope William, he finally agreed to see Cardinal Whittier. "Hello Peter," said William.

"William, tomorrow is Josip's great show. You're going to have to show yourself at his conference."

"I don't want to," said William. "I am quite embarrassed. I feel like a noted scientist I once knew. He was so in love with one of his hypothesis he refused to believe it wouldn't work. He wasted most of his younger years trying to prove it until finally admitting it wouldn't work. He felt he was a great scientist on the verge of receiving the Nobel Prize for his work. He felt it was just within his reach. It never happened. I too haughtily believed I was such a great Pope I would be canonized even before my death. I began believing I could cure the sick." William laughed at himself. "I saw myself walking on water."

"William, be sensible," said Peter. "You were not that way at all. Sure, sometimes you became a little conceited but I can assure you nearly every Pope I knew suffered from that illness once in a while. Thankfully Rosalie and your two sons brought you back down to earth."

"I have to resign, Peter. I am truly a fraud."

Cardinal Whittier said, "William, do you know what a fraud is? A fraud is in imposter; a trickster, a phony who purposely creates a scam to fool others. Did you do that?"

"It makes no difference..."

Peter interrupted William, "Answer me, yes or no. Did you create a scam? Did you hire a magician or arrange some other scheme to make those phony ballots?"

"Peter, it makes..."

Peter interrupted again, "Answer me, William. Yes or no. Did you create those phony ballots?"

"No."

Breathing a sigh Peter said, "See. There you are. You are not a phony; a trickster or imposter."

Pope William looked down at his slippers. "I have no choice, Peter. I have to resign whether or not I created those ballots."

"Yes, that's probably true unless I can find out how this predicament came about. My secretary is trying to locate Perez's detective now. I am determined to find out all the facts. I will not let this lie. More and more I feel it was a miracle that you were elected and I will prove it."

William looked at his trusted friend, "Peter, you are a good friend, but don't let this problem pull you down too. Josip will attack you next."

"I can take care of myself, don't you worry about me." Cardinal Whittier stood up. "Okay, tomorrow morning I am coming by to take you to Perez's show. Be ready at eight."

"Thanks, Peter."

Cardinal Whittier yelled into the next room, "Rosalie, don't you go packing for Illinois yet."

Cardinal Whittier and Pope William entered the Basilica from a side entrance and quietly sat down. As could be imagined, Cardinal Perez arranged his conference in St. Peter's Basilica with a great show of solemnity. Nearly two hundred Cardinals, archbishops and bishops were assembled, quietly whispering speculation about the content of the conference. Pope William wore plain tan slacks and white shirt, not his unusual black attire he always insisted on wearing. Cardinal Perez, dressed in his most elegant red apparel, walked to the front of the group.

Appearing most pious Cardinal Perez said, "Brethren in Christ, let us pray that I, God's most humble servant, may do Him homage in this unusual and sorrowful conference. It is with great sadness I bring this message to you. I have prayed reverently and fervently that this day would not come to pass. But it has and I must bring its message to light.

"Our Pope William, whom I have grown to love and respect, has had an unusual circumstance placed upon his innocent shoulders. I want to emphasize most vehemently it was not instigated by our beloved Pope William. I trust him most implicitly that it happened through no accountability of our Pope. But it has happened none the less.

"As you all know, I had a respected detective and fervent practicing Catholic review and discern how William could be elected. And as you know, we did not place William's name on our ballot. I might add, my detective worked diligently for over six months without accepting any monetary compensation."

At that statement, Father O'Rourke took notice.

Cardinal Perez held up a large envelope before the group. "Here, my fellow brethren, is the proof. I have only thirty-seven ballots to demonstrate the deceptiveness of the fraudulent election. Since there are so many of us I will have to exhibit its contents and how the deception was accomplished to one small group at a time."

Cardinal Perez, with a great show of pomp, made an elaborate display of the ballot transformation to each small group. Notably Pope William remained seated. After an hour of immense pageantry, the almost comic affair ended.

"Josip," Cardinal Whittier said, "Did your detective friend find out who did it?"

"No, and I begged him repeatedly to find out that bit of information for me. He is still working on it but he said it was cleverly done by some expert."

"I still think it is a miracle," said Cardinal Kwan.

Cardinal Perez said, "I prayed it would be a miracle too, Aiden, but the proof is here."

Cardinals Signorelli and Stanlove looked at each other questioning Cardinal Perez's words.

Pope William stood up, "Gentlemen, it is not necessary to find out who did it. It was done and the result is I cannot remain as your pope. Cardinal Whittier will explain to me the procedure of resignation. I will deliver it as soon as possible." Saying that the humbled Pope left the Basilica.

"NO, NO!" said several Cardinals and bishops. "Wait, we need more of an explanation. Who did it?"

Cardinal Raymundo said, "Josip, I want to speak to this detective of yours. I want to see what he did and how he did it."

Sadly Josip said, "I'm sorry. He had to leave for the United States. He's been called as an expert witness in a Grand Jury. He'll be sequestered in the States for quite a while."

Quietly to himself Cardinal Whittier said, "How convenient." Out loud he said, "Josip, it sounds like an unfinished task if you ask me. I'm going to call Mr. Candelo's office and find out where and when he can be reached. We must find out who did it."

Nervously Cardinal Perez said, "I already have a call in for him to contact me as soon as he has some free time."

"Fine, I will put a call in for him, too."

"There's no need, Peter. I'm taking care of that matter."

Cardinal Whittier said again, "I will still try to contact him."

Cardinal Perez said, "Brethren, you can return to your rooms and we can begin our Conclave as soon as William's resignation is received. Since there has been such confusion and we have so many new Cardinals, I would like to place myself at your disposal and would gladly accept a nomination as Pope. With my experience, I would quickly give our worried flock a continuity they so desperately desire. I would sincerely attempt to continue the good work Pope William has begun."

Cardinal Di Metri whispered in Cardinal Whittier's ear, "What a pompous ass." Cardinal Whittier nodded in agreement.

Cardinal Perez said, "Let's close with a prayer that the Holy Spirit will guide us through this trying situation. When I receive the resignation tomorrow we can begin the election procedure." Josip was greatly surprised no one stayed to pray with him. They all left before he even started prayers.

Cardinal Perez rushed to his office. His secretary, Father O'Rourke, was waiting at his desk. "Josip, is it going to work out like you desire?"

"Definitely," said Josip. "The only little item I want to work out it that he resigns as Pope. Then we can begin voting. That way his election will be recorded as a fluke. The years will let his term in office fade from everyone's memory. Nearly every pope resigning did so under suspicious circumstances. His edicts will be eradicated from all Papal history and soon will be ignored or reversed. And the good part, Lawrence, is that since I will be Pope, I can reverse those idiot edicts with a great display of sadness."

"Is there any possibility Edwardo will tell who or why it was done?" asked Father O'Rourke.

"I don't care if he does or doesn't. I don't even care who did it or why it was done but it was done and that's good enough for me. I do have to contact Edwardo, though. That meddling Whittier wants to muddy up the waters."

"What does he want to do?"

"He wants to contact Candelo. He wants to ask him a bunch of questions about who did it and why. I made up some reason why he can't be contacted at this time. I don't think he believed me. God, I hate that man."

Father O'Rourke said, "We could contact Gina and ask her to spend some time with Mr. Candelo. She has helped us before convincing men to see our way."

"Yes, that slut has assisted us before and she's not too expensive. First call Edwardo and see if we can convince him to refuse any calls from Whittier – without costing us any more money. I would hate to have to ask Luigi for more cash. Then call Gina."

"Did Edwardo say who staged the election?"

"I didn't want to know. I guess I should have found out."

"But that person might tell," said Lawrence.

"I don't care. I don't care," said Josip. "It was done and it was not a ridiculous miracle. That's the important thing. I can't see God coming down and putting His finger on a cop."

"I still worry about Edwardo messing things up for you, my friend."

"So what. I didn't do anything underhanded. I am only saying what Edwardo told me. He can tell anybody anything he wants. And since this dumb heathen hasn't practiced Catholicism since his childhood, he couldn't care less about what goes on here in the Vatican. He was well paid."

"I wondered why you said he worked for free."

Josip said, "I didn't mean to say that. I got carried away. Who cares? Anyway I don't think the one who actually rigged the election will ever come forward. They were able to witness the results of their little joke and have a laugh. Also there may be criminal charges I'm sure."

"Maybe," said Lawrence doubtfully.

"And I might add Lawrence, there will be a little stipend for you, my faithful servant. I think I may also see an elevation for you. I will need a trustworthy and dedicated cardinal in my reign as pope."

"Thank you, your Eminence."

"I've got to see the resignation before the Conclave meets to elect the next pope – me."

Father O'Rourke said, "Do you believe they'll elect you, Josip?"

"With the confusion and chaos all around us, I'm the only obvious choice. Those new Cardinals William appointed have no idea who to vote for. I've been molding them into lambs heading for slaughter. I've talked to each one of them individually and I promised them nice assignments to countries of their choice. Ha! Once I'm elected I will probably forget what I said, but no matter. As Pope, Lawrence, you and I will pick some nice countries to visit. Start thinking now about where you'd like to go."

"Josip, it sounds too good to be true."

"Trust me, Lawrence, it's going to happen."

CHAPTER THIRTY

Cardinal Whittier knocked on the door to Pope William's private quarters. Rosalie was deep in gathering their belongings for an expected trip to the states. The family was preparing for their departure from the Vatican. She opened the door, letting Peter in.

"Hello, Cardinal," she said.

"Hello, Rosalie. How is William today? He didn't come over to his office and I wondered how he was taking all this drama."

Rosalie said, "He pretty downcast. I think the hardest part is his guilt. He doesn't feel guilty for accepting the nomination, just for his taking himself too seriously."

William walked into the room. "Hello Peter."

"Why aren't you in your office?" said Peter.

"Why should I? I've filled out my resignation for you. I am no longer the Pope. We're packing to go somewhere although I don't know where. We can't go back to Peoria. We'd be too embarrassed. I guess it'd be more correct to say I'd be too embarrassed."

"Why is that, William?" said Peter. "We've been all through this. You didn't create the election results. We still don't know why it happened. What's your problem?"

William said, "My guilt, Peter, my guilt. It's how I reacted to the whole affair. It's like I told you the other day. I became narcissistic, vain, and even egotistical. I imagined myself as St. William. You know what else? I didn't address any of the world's problems, like pollution, or the rich countries ignoring the poor or rulers killing their citizens or starving people. All I thought about was my little agendas. "

Cardinal Whittier threw up his hands, "Oh hogwash. William you weren't that bad. I would have thoroughly chastised you if you became that arrogant."

"Peter, what can I do? What can my family do?"

"William, I've got a plan. When you resign, I've got it all planned out. You're not leaving Rome. You aren't even leaving the Vatican. You and your family are staying right here, maybe not in this apartment but on the Vatican grounds."

William said, "Are you serious?"

"Deadly serious."

"I don't know how that could happen."

Peter said, "Trust me. We will let Perez play out his little game and then we'll spring it on him."

"I'd like to believe it, Peter. Not just for my sake but for Rosalie and the boys. They don't even want to go out of the apartment."

"William, it'll work out just fine. Rosalie and the boys will be able to walk around Vatican grounds with heads held high. Now, tell Rosalie to pack just for a local move – probably to a different apartment. And get David and Charles out there to play some soccer. The head gardener even misses seeing the boys trying to repair plants they knocked over. He said he had to laugh watching them straighten bent branches, all the while looking around to see if anyone saw them."

"Peter, if you can make that happen, then you are a miracle worker."

"Now, as much as I hate to say it, you will have to resign. We can't change that. I have arranged for you and your family to move to an apartment set aside for special visitors and guests of the Vatican. It has several rooms so you won't be crowded. I contacted Mr. Candelo's secretary and she'll have him call me as soon as he returns from a short trip. He's not in the States. She doesn't know why Josip said he was unavailable. I think I know why Josip said it."

"Peter, you're going through a lot of trouble for me."

"Why not? We people from Illinois must stick together."

William Meier handed Peter his official resignation. "I guess this is it?"

"Since I am still officially the pope's secretary – until the new pope relieves me - I've arranged to hold the Conclave tomorrow since all the Cardinals are still here in Rome. I've also arranged housing for the archbishops and bishops since they can't attend the Conclave."

"Yes, I forgot about that," said William.

Cardinal Whittier said," I don't mean to rush you but I also have contacted some of the staff to help you and Rosalie relocate to your new residence."

William asked, "Does Josip really have the election sewed up? Will he be the next pope?"

"William, not in a million years. The new Pope may even reduce his position."

"Do you have any idea who will be the next Pope?"

Cardinal Whittier smiled, "Like you once said, probably some old Cardinal. Things are in such a confused state they will elect someone not expected to live very long. Until we get reorganized they will elect an old timer not anticipated to be around long enough to make any immediate changes."

"Do you think he'll invalidate my edicts?"

Cardinal Whittier said, "I don't think so. While most of the older Cardinals hate to admit it, your edicts have been quite popular. Look at the increase in attendance worldwide and even here in Rome where attendance is notoriously low. Tithing has increased as have Catholics wanting to become clergymen and clergywomen. It's also quite strange but we've had an increase from ministers of other denominations desirous to join us and become priests. I don't think those edicts will be nullified."

"Maybe I've done some good."

"William, quit throwing yourself under the bus."

"You're right, Peter," said William. "I'm going to trust you – and God – and let whatever happens happen."

"Great. Now, the Conclave meets tomorrow. Let's see who gets elected and how many days it takes."

"Any favorites?" asked William.

"I can tell you I'm voting for Balino but Cesario is probably the favorite."

William smiled, "How about you?"

"Gracious me, no. I'm too American and too young."

"Can you vote for yourself?"

"No. We're not supposed to."

Cardinal Whittier's assistant knocked on the door. "Cardinal, several staff members are here to facilitate the Pope's move."

“Show them in,” said William. “No use waiting.”

Cardinal Whittier said, “Now you and Rosalie just relax and let these gentlemen take care of everything. You, Rosalie and the boys come with me. I’ll show you your new home – for the time being.”

“Once again, thank you Peter.”

“It’s been my pleasure and it will continue to be.”

CHAPTER THIRTY-ONE

It took a few extra days for the Conclave to be held but it convened within four days of Pope William's official resignation. In an unprecedented occurrence, a nearly unanimous decision was reached. Peter Whittier's name appeared on almost every ballot. All the Cardinals agreed the name written was the one they had chosen. There was no miraculous, mysterious problem this time. The young and newly elected Cardinals were extremely exuberant with the choice, not even considering Cardinal Perez. The Catholics of Illinois were happy too since they again had a Pope from their state. Truly North America was happy a Pope had been chosen from their continent. Cardinal Whittier, though, was dumfounded.

"Oh my God," was all he could say.

William Meier was also thrilled to say the least. "That makes a lot more sense," he said. Rosalie, although still at a loss to explain the turn of events, was happy too.

"Cardinal Whittier has sure taken care of us," she said to William. "I still wonder where we'll end up."

Bill said, "I wonder what name he'll choose?"

"We'll find out tomorrow," said Rosalie. "At least he can speak Italian. He helped me a lot getting conversant in the language."

William said, "It's sad what happened to Cardinal Perez."

"I know," said Rosalie. "Dominic came by again to play soccer with the boys. I'm so glad the boys are out mixing with the deacons and young priests again. He told me Josip went ballistic when he didn't receive one vote for pope. Well, he did receive one vote. It was assumed his own."

"Did you hear what happened to him?" said William.

"No."

"He was last seen walking along the Tiber River. It is not believed he committed suicide because nobody has been found. They said he was extremely remorseful. Cardinal Balino said he asked if he could just remain on the Vatican as a grounds keeper. Salvatore told him it was okay. Josip also revoked his vows."

"Sad how the desire for power can corrupt," said William. "Look what it was doing to me."

"Bill, you were doing okay. Peter and I were watching you and your moves. We would have brought you down to Earth. Oh my gosh! I can't call him Peter anymore. He's a Pope."

"Dad," said Charles, rushing into the room. "Guess what name Peter chose?

"I can't. What is it?"

"You won't believe it. He chose to be Pope William the second. That's pretty neat. Oh, and he wants to meet with you and Mom next Monday. He said it is very important."

"What on earth for?" said Rosalie.

Bill said, "Maybe to tell me what he's going to do with us. We can't just go on living off the Vatican. We've got to do something to earn our keep."

"I know," said Rosalie.

"At least the boys are once again happily breaking bushes."

"Dad!" said Charles in a moan.

CHAPTER THIRTY-TWO

William and Rosalie timidly approached the door to the Pope's office. They were very familiar with the office. It was once the office of Pope William the First. A very large man sat in a seat across from the Pope's secretary, Father Thiel.

"Hello, Father," said William. "It's good to see you again."

"Same here," said Father.

"Come in, come in," said the new Pope William. The new Pope didn't even let his secretary escort the couple in. He ushered them into his office himself. "Sit down, folks. I'm sure you remember the furnishings. I've no intention of changing anything,"

"Your holiness, I'm honored and slightly bewildered by your choosing the name William as your name."

"William, to me you are a saint in the making. Wait until you hear what Mr. Candelo has to say. Father, send Mr. Candelo in."

The very large man the couple saw in the waiting room entered Pope William's office.

"Mr. Candelo, meet the world famous Pope William the first."

"Your Holiness, please don't call me that," said William.

"Then you William, don't call me 'Your Holiness'. Call me Peter," said the Pope.

"I can't do that."

"Yes you can. So, Mr. Candelo, tell William your story."

The big man took a deep breath. "Well folks, I heard what happened to you. It didn't bother me at first but it grew on me after I heard what they did to you. Or should I say what Mr. Perez did to you with my information."

Mr. Candelo seemed awed by the presence of the Pope and the people in the office. "Mr. Perez asked me specifically how your election could be faked. I was surprised he didn't ask me how it was done, just how it <u>could</u> be done. He paid me a lot of money to do it."

William and Rosalie sat astonished.

"So I had my chemists figure out a way to do it. So they did. I assumed my task wasn't completed but I took my partial results of how it could be done to Mr. Perez. I wanted to tell him some unexpected findings. He didn't care. I expected him to send me on my way to find out who actually did the deed. He said he didn't care about that either. He threw the money at me and told me to get out. I thought it strange but I left. I took my money and bought a new car. Almost immediately my secretary said Mr. Perez was trying to contact me but I wasn't too anxious to talk to him. I figured I'd let him wait. But I was curious myself how it was done so I had my chemists continue working on it and find out more about it. That they did. But before I could tell anybody about our final results Mr. Perez said Cardinal Whittier…er the Pope here… was trying to contact me but I shouldn't talk to him. I wondered why. Then he sent some whore… excuse me Mrs. Meier… to influence me like I was some kind of bum. Now I was piss…I mean angry. I knew then what I had to do, especially after I heard what happened to you, sir. So last week I contacted the Pope here and told him the story. I told him what my chemists had discovered. He said I had to tell you. So here I am."

"Okay, Edwardo. Tell them what you found."

"Well, here goes. My guys told me that they were determined to find out what kind of ink was used to create the fake ballots. They scraped and scraped the writing, trying to get a sample of the ink to analyze. They scraped it until they made a hole in the paper. I guess you could say the ink never scraped off. It seemed to be suspended a millimeter or less above the paper. When they wore a hole through the paper, the ink or writing disappeared. It was like it was never there. My guys couldn't explain it. I tried to tell this to Mr. Perez but he wasn't interested. I wanted to tell Mr. Perez it was some kind of magic but he never gave me a chance to explain. It sounded kinda spooky to me. So after hearing what was happening to you guys, I eventually got to talk to the Pope here. That's it."

William and Rosalie sat completely dumbfounded. "What's he saying?" asked William. "What am I hearing?"

"William," said the Pope, "I think you know. I believe it was a miracle. I truly think God chose you to be Pope."

"I don't understand what this means," said William. "Are you saying I shouldn't have resigned?"

"Probably not but it is too late. What's done is done. But here's what I propose. Remember when I said I had a plan?"

"Yes."

"Well, it goes like this," said the Pope. "I want you to accept a position as deacon. I'm going to put you on the fast track to become a priest, a bishop, a cardinal and ... who knows? William, it was truly a miracle when you were elected. I am going to make it possible for you to again be elected Pope, or at least have a second chance to be elected. You would be the first man in Church history to be elected Pope twice. It would be with your approval, though. What do you say?"

"I don't know what to say."

Pope William said, "You're an intelligent man. It wouldn't take you long to complete the studies for the priesthood with me coaching you. Now that I am Pope, I can pull strings to hasten things. Now what do you say?"

"Rosalie," said William, "Am I hearing him right?"

Rosalie sat in silence.

"Peter, can you really do this?"

"I'm Pope, remember?"

"Where would I live? Where would my family live?"

"Exactly where you are now. I will start you tomorrow with your studies."

"But Peter, I'm a married man."

"For goodness sake, William," said Peter. "Have you forgotten your edict already regarding celibacy?

Both your edicts have become quite popular."

"Peter, I..."

"Just say thank you and prepare to begin studying tomorrow. I'll make your class fast but not easy. Good Lord I'm glad I thought of this solution. What do you think of it, Rosalie?"

"Peter," said Rosalie, "I think you should be named a saint."

"Thank you, my dear. Now, William. Remember this. I can't assure you that you would be elected Pope, just that you'll soon be a Cardinal and the possibility would exist."

Father Thiel stuck his head in the door. "Sister Ann is on the phone."

"Oh my gosh. Get her number and tell her I'll call her in a few minutes. Darn you William. Leaving me with Sister Ann and that unfinished business. What do I tell her?"

"Tell her the door is still closed on women's ordination but closed doors can always be reopened. Maybe the next Pope may open the door."

"Brilliant, William. Brilliant.

William and Rosalie returned to their apartment by way of the Basilica. On their knees in the large edifice they thanked God for the turn of events.

Four years have passed. Cardinal William Meier sat in the Sistine Chapel with 107 other Cardinals. Pope William the second's sudden death left a large hole in Cardinal William Meier's heart. There would never be another man whose friendship would be as valued as the late Pope's. The Pope's constant urging and teaching made possible the rapid rise of William Meier to Cardinal. The ordination of women was always on the late Pope's mind. All knew the day was coming but no one could say when.

Rosalie eventually had one of her paintings placed in the museum, though it was in a far corner. Both boys were chosen for the soccer team. Cardinal William Meier had not made it to Pope again but he was still young and time was in his favor. The story of William Meier's rise and fall and rise again was always on the lips of the Vatican tour guides. Once again, the old saying was true. God moves in mysterious ways.

THE END

About the Author

John retired as a district sales manager in 2000 after nearly 29 years with the same employer. He has always wanted to write and now in his retirement years he has the time to pursue his interest. John has traveled all fifty states and most Canadian provinces gathering material for stories.

His hobbies include model trains, guitar, singing in the church choir and helping family and friends with home improvement projects. His younger years included running eight Marathons and belonging to two tennis leagues. His first novel was a SCI FI *Seeking a Perfect World* published in 2014.

John lives in Iowa with his wife Clara.

CPSIA information can be obtained
at www.ICGtesting.com
Printed in the USA
FFOW04n0725051016
28204FF

9 781506 903064